BOOKER & FITCH MY

CW00348805

# MURDER
## for
# Beginners

## LIZ HEDGECOCK   PAULA HARMON

WHITE
RHINO
BOOKS

ISBN-13: 979-8374387377

*To our husbands, Stephen and Mark,*
*with thanks for keeping our glasses topped up*
*while we plot!*

# CHAPTER 1

'Hrrraaaarrrghh!'

Jade Fitch sat bolt upright in her bed, white and shaking. It took her a few seconds to collect herself: the sensation of a hand gripping her shoulder and a stern voice saying 'Caught up with you at last, Fitch,' had been so very real.

Her heart banged in her chest. This wasn't helped by her unfamiliar surroundings. The duvet she knew, with its pattern of bright pink and orange splashy flowers on a cream background. The rest of the room – plain magnolia walls, thin cream curtains, a bare bulb dangling from the ceiling, an oak veneer bedside table, with matching chest of drawers and wardrobe, none quite straight – was both alien and not what she would have chosen in a million years. She regarded it with disdain. 'As soon as I've got the shop in order…' she muttered to herself.

She glanced at the clock on the bedside table. 7:30, it said, in large, glowing green numerals.

Jade sighed. 'No time like the present.' She swung her legs out of bed and padded towards the purple terry dressing gown hanging on the back of the door.

After a mug of strong tea and two slices of toast with blackcurrant jam, she felt ready to tackle the shower. The landlord's instructions regarding it, while sketchy, had been pretty straightforward: make sure the immersion is on, switch shower on, turn dial to desired temperature. However, in the week or so that Jade had inhabited the flat, the best the shower had managed was a lukewarm, malevolent trickle. Jade had tried various tactics – following the instructions, turning the dial to maximum, attempting reverse psychology by setting it to minimum, insulting it – and nothing had worked.

'I will not be defeated by you,' she murmured, eyeing it.

The shower appeared completely unmoved.

Jade followed the instructions and the usual tepid stream materialised. 'Maybe I should ring the landlord and get it replaced,' she said, as if talking to a friend. 'It's probably worn out.'

As if by magic, the water pressure increased and the stream became appreciably warmer. Jade cast off her dressing gown and jumped in before the appliance had a change of heart. When she had finished, she turned off the shower and patted it on its side. 'I'm glad we understand each other.'

She took care in selecting her clothes for the day. On one hand, she would be moving things around, so flowing skirts and floating scarves would get in the way. On the other, she had her reputation as the proprietor of Hazeby-on-Wyvern's premier (she hoped) crystal and magic shop to establish. Eventually she chose a long skirt patterned in purple and black, slit to the knee for ease of movement, teamed with a short-sleeved black top with a neckline which she considered just about appropriate for daywear. She added a black beaded choker, and coaxed her mass of curly hair into two low bunches. She laced up her Doc Martens, nodded at herself in the mirror, and went downstairs to the shop.

She surveyed it with dismay. Granted, the walls were now a beautiful midnight blue, sprinkled with silver stars, and the shelves were more or less straight, but there was so much left to unpack. She hadn't even started on the window display – the big picture window was currently covered with brown paper – and the shop was due to have its grand opening in two days. She shrugged. 'Let's get on with it,' she said, out loud. 'No one else will do it, will they?' She switched on the lights, then hunted for the box she had labelled *Fabric/Drapes* and pulled out a large black velvet cloth.

An hour and a half later, Jade was reasonably pleased with her handiwork. She had draped the cloth to her satisfaction and set up two shelving units on either side of the window. One was filled with crystals – from boxes of small ones to a couple of largish geodes which had made Jade wince when she pressed the Buy Now button – as well as pendants and silver jewellery. The other shelving unit contained incense sticks, candles, miniature cauldrons, crystal balls and packs of tarot cards. Dreamcatchers of varying sizes dangled at the top of the window, and in the middle, on stands, were spell books, books on the law of attraction, books of magic tricks, and CDs of panpipe music. 'Something for everyone,' said Jade, surveying it. 'How does it look from the front?'

Carefully she climbed into the window and picked at the sticky tape holding the brown paper in place. She was so absorbed in her task that a sharp rap at the window made her overbalance and clutch the left-hand shelf for support. It wobbled, and several packs of tarot cards fell over.

Jade righted the shelf and glared at the person who had disturbed her. He was an older man with brushed-back grey hair, dressed in what Jade deemed an unnecessarily smart manner. He wore a pale-yellow shirt with a navy cravat tucked into it, red trousers, and a tweed jacket which she was prepared to swear would have elbow patches. Under his arm was a largish box, with multicoloured square stickers placed in a seemingly random pattern.

'What?' she said, still frowning.

The man made stabbing motions at the window, his mouth moving, but she couldn't hear a thing.

'I'll come out,' she said, jerking a thumb at the door, and fished her keys from her pocket.

When Jade got outside, she couldn't resist pausing to take in the window. 'Excellent,' she said, beaming.

'I can't say I agree,' the man replied.

'We'll have to agree to disagree then, won't we,' said Jade. 'May I ask who you are?'

'You may.' The man extended the hand unencumbered by the parcel. 'Freddy Stott. I own the shop next door: Yesteryear Antiquities. I take it you're new.'

Jade debated whether to shake the proffered hand, and decided it was probably rude not to. Freddy Stott immediately exerted a strong grip which Jade returned, thankful for all the arm-wrestling contests she had won in pubs over the years. 'I've been here a week,' she said, releasing her grip. 'I'm opening the shop in two days.'

'It's a good thing I caught you, then,' said Freddy, his grimace of pain transforming into an ingratiating smile. 'I wouldn't want you to get off on the wrong foot. People are . . . particular.'

'Are they,' said Jade, grimly.

'Oh yes. Hazeby-on-Wyvern has won the best market town award five years running. The locals and our visitors are very discerning, and we can't afford to lower the tone.' He gazed sorrowfully at Jade's shop window. 'Your predecessor Emily had such beautiful window displays. So tasteful. Beautiful fabrics, and such lovely cushions.'

'Where's Emily now?' asked Jade, though she didn't care about tasteful Emily's lovely cushions one bit.

An expression of deep regret spread across Freddy's face. 'I fear circumstances did not permit her to continue with the shop. Cash flow...' He waved a careless hand in the air. 'It's so difficult to strike a balance.'

'Ah, so Emily went out of business because she wasn't making a living from the shop,' said Jade. 'If tasteful window displays couldn't save her, let's see what mine will do.'

She leaned towards a young woman with a pushchair who was regarding a book of spells with a wistful air. 'Crystal Dreams will be opening in two days, pet. I can save you a copy of that book.'

The woman managed a nervous nod, then, conscious of Jade and Freddy's eyes on her, said 'Come on, Noah, time for elevenses' to the pushchair and hurried off.

The corners of Freddy's mouth curled upwards.

'Best not to scare the customers away… I'm afraid I didn't catch your name.'

'Jade. Jade Fitch.'

'Jade Fitch,' Freddy repeated, rolling Jade's name around his mouth like a mid-price wine. 'You did say Fitch, didn't you?'

'I did,' said Jade, wondering what was coming next.

'Well, Jade Fitch, I had better get on. I have a business to run, and hopefully, so do you.'

'Don't worry about me, Freddy,' said Jade. Her fingers twitched with the urge to smack him, and she clenched her fists.

'Jolly good,' said Freddy, sneering at her window display. 'I must say that there's one good thing about having you next door.'

'Oh yes? What's that?'

'My wife Wendy was always bringing home bits and bobs from Emily's shop. It got to the point where you could barely move in our house for the elegant clutter of throw pillows and embroidery kits, and I had to put my foot down. Now you're here, I'll be able to rest easy.'

'I wouldn't be too sure,' said Jade, drawing herself up to her full height.

Freddy made a noise like a sheep, which puzzled Jade until she realised it was supposed to be a laugh. 'Oh, really?'

'I have no idea whether your Wendy is interested in what my shop has to offer,' said Jade. 'However, if I catch you being rude about my shop, or putting it into anyone's head that it lowers the tone of this place, I may have to take measures.' She tapped the glass in front of the spell book and gave Freddy a knowing look.

Freddy stepped back as if Jade had hit him, which she found immensely gratifying. 'No need for that,' he snapped.

'Fitch by name,' said Jade, as he turned to go, and allowed herself a little giggle as he stepped into his shop. *That's shown him what's what*, she thought, brushing the imaginary dust of him off her hands. *If that's the worst this town has in store, this should be an easy ride.*

She surveyed the street and caught the eye of a few people, who quickly appeared engrossed in a shop window or a bus timetable. 'The grand opening of Crystal Dreams is in two days!' she called. 'Come and see what the shop has to offer.' She fancied that one or two people looked thoughtful.

*Time for a cup of tea.* She stepped back for one last admiring glance at her window display, and strode inside.

# CHAPTER 2

'Shall I take *this* one?'

Fi's fourteen-year-old son Dylan stood in the doorway of the barge, piece of toast in one hand, reaching towards the umbrella stand with the other. It contained items forgotten by customers over the years, which Fi kept in case their owners returned. Dylan snatched up one that might have belonged to a city gent.

'I thought umbrellas were uncool, like raincoats, sensible shoes, and gloves in winter,' said Fi. 'How will you carry it to school while riding a bicycle? I know you're tall, but it's still half your height. And why today, when it's finally stopped raining and you don't need one? For the last five days you've come home looking like you've swum because "only kids wear coats".'

It was risky to suggest a teenager was an idiot first

thing in the morning, but first thing in the morning Fi hadn't had enough coffee to develop any patience, and today she was on edge.

Dylan, however, ignored her jibes and answered the one question he judged relevant. 'I'll tie it across my back,' he said, as if that was the most obvious thing in the world.

'Like a ninja sword?'

'Yeah, Mum,' said Dylan, voice heavy with sarcasm. He rolled his eyes. 'Anyway, I've got a belt to strap it on.' Shoving the toast into his mouth, he put words to action.

Fi watched him struggle as expressionlessly as she could, torn between helping him, so there was a chance of the umbrella staying put, and telling him to leave the umbrella behind, since it would slip halfway to school if not before and make him wish he'd never taken it. But she hadn't the energy to deal with any of the responses, either: *I can do it myself, Mum, I'm not a baby; aw, Mum, you never let me do anything; do you think I'm an idiot, Mum?* He'd just have to learn for himself. 'Seriously though, Dylan, what's it for?'

'Drama. I *told* you.'

He hadn't.

'Of course it is.' Fi looked at the clock. She was five feet seven, but her son already overtopped her by three inches, making her feel vaguely ridiculous when she admonished him. 'You'll be late. Stuart will arrive any second. Don't stab anyone accidentally with that umbrella, or yourself. I'm not sure where it came from. It might be a secret agent's and maybe its tip or ferrule or whatever it's called was once dipped in an untraceable poison.'

Dylan rolled his eyes again and ruffled her hair, which indicated affectionate tolerance. 'I'm not six, Mum. See ya!' He went through the door, collected his bicycle from its store on the deck of the boat and wheeled it across the gangplank to the towpath. So far, the umbrella was staying put, but it was only a matter of time. She heard him call out: 'Morning, Stuart!'

'Morning, Dylan,' came Stuart's voice. 'Is it fancy-dress day? Do you need sponsorship? What are you going as? A ninja warrior or a secret agent?'

Fi smirked at Dylan's imagined response and went to greet Stuart. He had doubtless marched to the barge as if the muddy towpath was a busy street in Canary Wharf, since that was what he did. He was wearing a dark-blue suit and shiny brown shoes, now mud-spattered, and carrying the sort of briefcase that would have matched Dylan's city-gent umbrella very well. Fi always felt that Stuart had been born in the wrong era and longed to wear a bowler hat too. He'd only recently stopped wearing a tie.

'Morning, Fi.'

'Morning, Stuart. Coffee or tea?'

'Oh, I—'

'Hang on, Mum!' Dylan skidded back on his bicycle and after rummaging in a pocket, shoved a crumpled piece of paper at her. 'Don't forget this. They need it tomorrow. With the deposit. Everyone's going. See ya!'

He wheeled around and sped off.

Fi opened the piece of paper. 'It's dated two weeks ago,' she said. 'Another flaming school trip "to support his drama GCSE". Two hundred flipping quid. Fifty pounds by tomorrow or he can't go.'

'Tell you what,' said Stuart, 'I know where your kitchen is. I'll make you a coffee, shall I? You go and sit down.'

'Is it too early for gin?'

'I hope that umbrella won't kill him.'

'Hmmm,' said Fi. 'It'll save me the bother when he gets home.'

\*\*\*

Half an hour later, they were sitting at Fi's kitchen table in the private quarters of the barge. There wasn't room for two people to sit side by side with laptops and paperwork in the area which she referred to as her study. There was more space in the main part of the barge where the books were, but Fi's Monday assistant Geraldine was unpacking boxes and cataloguing things on the shared drive, and Fi didn't want her to overhear how the financial situation was.

It wasn't desperate, not yet, but the profit margins seemed to decrease by the month. Somehow, on a deeply illogical level, she didn't want the books to hear either. It was bad enough that the barge could. She had to get a grip.

'A new bilge pump won't cost much,' said Stuart.

'No, but we need a new, more efficient, more sustainable heating solution – solar panels could work, but goodness knows how long it'll take to recoup the cost and I'm not sure I have the funds. *Coralie*'s deck needs repainting and her hull needs re-tarring, which means paying to get her into a dry dock. Mooring fees have gone up, parking fees for the car have gone up and it needs a service anyway, or possibly replacement. I ought to pay Geraldine more, and I'd like to employ her or someone else for another day, so that I occasionally have some time off. Dylan's growing so fast I'm beginning to wonder if he's filling his shoes with compost. The amount of food he can put away is staggering. Flaming school trips and uniform and fundraising sponsorship every five minutes. Not to mention the main business of getting in bestsellers which will make a definite income without forgetting my goal – to find unloved books and guide them to a new home. Then if *Coralie*'s out of the water for any time, I have to find another way of managing the business. And there's something else I've forgotten.' Fi could hear herself becoming hysterical and put her head in her hands. 'What is it?'

'The licence fee for serving drinks on the towpath,' said Stuart, checking a list on his tablet.

'Not *on* the towpath,' objected Fi. 'On the grass *beyond* the towpath. And it's only in the warmer months. And it's nothing more exciting than tea, coffee and cold drinks. And it's not even me who's selling them. I'm just using the space outside the bookshop and putting up a gazebo. Willow's Wagon is doing the actual catering. The council acts as if I'm planning to set up a nightclub. Maybe I should.'

She took a deep swig of coffee. 'Sometimes I wonder what life would be like if I hadn't given up that city job. I'd have a swish house with plenty of space for Dylan to hang out with his friends. I'd have a wardrobe full of the latest fashions, we'd take foreign holidays...'

'Dylan doesn't complain, does he? And if he does, it's because he's fourteen and if you let him do and have whatever he wanted, he'd *still* complain. You took me on as your accountant four years ago and now you're one of my best friends. You had to get away from that life.'

'Yes. I did.'

'And you needed something new.'

'Yes, I did. I just don't think it's working. The money I invested is evaporating.'

'Your dream is sound, Fi,' said Stuart. 'With a bit

14

of jiggery-pokery, chiefly marketing, the book barge could do very well. This is a popular tourist town: the Wyvern has plenty of river-cruise ships coming up and down, the council is getting better at advertising the place, things are in your favour. Once word really gets out that there's a quirky bookshop which has everything from bestsellers to forgotten beauty manuals from the seventeenth century, with a cheerful, welcoming owner—'

'Humph.'

'Things will take off. I've gone through your accounts. You have enough leeway to do the maintenance. Can the dry dock wait till after the summer?'

'Yes.'

'Good. Then with a marketing strategy set out you could obtain the small amount of finance you need to improve your website and social media and increase advertising. Perhaps start a blog or a YouTube channel, which might attract revenue eventually. You have the skills to create an excellent marketing strategy and business plan, Fi.'

'Have I got the creativity to do the social media stuff? I did a business degree then I was corporate for twenty years. All the imagination has been squeezed out of me.'

'You had the imagination to set up a bookshop and the skills to run it successfully when you gave up the corporate life. Let the books work their magic on you.' Stuart wiggled his fingers as if casting a spell.

Fi laughed. Some of the gloom lifted. Five days of rain in summer, when business was usually fairly good, hadn't helped. Not to mention dealing with the shifting sands that were Dylan's adolescent moods. To be fair, he didn't complain about the tiny amount of private space that was his compared with his friends. Somehow, she'd find the two hundred pounds for the school trip, even if Dylan had to be warned that this was the last time he left it to the last minute to tell her, and on a practical level he would have to help with the deck painting.

'I always worry the council thinks I'm too gaudy for the town,' said Fi, sobering a little. 'A bit too fey. There was that hoo-hah not long ago about the takeaways using red paint when the town ought to be in traditional eighteenth-century colours. If people in the eighteenth century could have painted the town anything other than sludge green and black, it would have been twenty times more tasteless than anything Cheeky Chick'n could come up with nowadays.'

'I agree,' said Stuart, 'but even so, you're quite bland compared to the new place that's opening: Crystal Dreams. I went past it this morning. Very pretty display – stars, purple, sparkly things. I swear it said "spells for sale".'

'Is that the one that's taken the spot next to

Yesteryear Antiquities? Stars and sparkly things?' Fi laughed again. 'Old Freddy won't like that!' She stood up and put the kettle on. 'You've cheered me up no end, Stuart. If someone can sell sparkly things and spells in Hazeby-on-Wyvern, I can sell books. Let's finish these accounts, then you can help me brainstorm about my new, improved website.'

# CHAPTER 3

Jade gazed at the shop, satisfied. OK, so some shelves looked crammed while others were sparse, but she had stock and it was on the shelves. Crystals and healing items in one part of the shop, cauldrons and spell books in another, candles and incense near the till where she could keep an eye on them.

Her stomach growled in a way which Jade chose to interpret as approval, but also hunger. *Time for lunch.* She visualised the contents of the fridge and the three small cupboards that made up the flat's kitchenette. It didn't take long. *After all that hard work, I deserve more than a ham sandwich. And I don't mean a jam sandwich.*

She chuckled, pulled her bag from behind the counter and unlocked the shop door. *Anyway*, she thought, *I ought to explore the town and get to know my customers.*

*Assuming there are any*, said a nagging little voice inside her head.

*Of course there will be*, she told it. *What about the people who were listening earlier when I was talking to what's-his-name next door? Besides, this town is practically next to a stone circle. I bet there are more hippies and witchy types round here than you can shake a stick at. Maybe there's even druids.* She hugged herself at the thought of crowds of people, possibly wearing tie-dye garments, queueing up to buy amethyst pendants and chunky silver rings.

Her stomach rumbled again, this time with more of a warning tone. 'I'm going!' she said, laughing, and let herself out of the shop.

The first thing she did was look in the window of Yesteryear Antiquities. From what Freddy had said, she anticipated Chippendale chairs and Constable paintings. Instead she saw a large globe, open to reveal a cocktail cabinet, a phrenology head, and a tea set remarkable for its completeness, its hideousness, and the size of its price tag. *Discerning, eh.* Jade sniffed, then pushed open the door of the shop. A bell announced her arrival with a loud jangle.

She had expected Freddy to be at the counter, but he was nowhere to be seen. Instead, a young woman with long dark hair was filing her nails and talking, apparently to herself. 'That's what I said. I mean, you can't do a thing like that and then, you know, ghost people.' Jade realised she was wearing a Bluetooth earpiece. 'Don't mind me,' she said. 'Just browsing.'

The young woman, indeed, did not mind her. In fact, she didn't seem to see Jade. Jade found this refreshing, since she often felt more visible than the average person. Maybe it was her height, maybe it was her hair, maybe it was that her jewellery had a tendency to rattle.

She had moved further down the shop to inspect a beige phone, which she was sure was the model she had grown up with in the late seventies, when Freddy Stott pushed aside the curtain at the back of the shop and strode out like a pantomime villain.

'Oh,' he said, stopping short. 'It's you.'

'It is indeed,' said Jade, checking the price on the phone and reflecting that either it was surprisingly rare or Freddy was overcharging. 'I thought I'd pop in and discover what you're offering the fastidious inhabitants of the town.' She gazed around her. 'Quiet, isn't it?'

'It'll pick up after lunch,' said Freddy. 'Always does.'

Jade eyed him. 'Not during the lunch break?'

'Any time now,' said Freddy, rocking on the balls of his feet. 'Are you planning to buy that phone?'

'As I said, just looking,' said Jade.

'I don't encourage browsers. They get in the way of purchasers.'

'Oh, I'm sorry.' Jade stepped back, then called to the empty shop, 'Feel free to go ahead of me!' The young woman behind the till jumped, glared at her for a moment, then returned to filing her nails.

Jade faced Freddy again. 'I think I've seen enough.'

'Excellent,' said Freddy. 'Mind your head on the way out. Wouldn't want you to damage anything.'

Jade smirked and made what she hoped was a dignified exit. As she pulled open the door she heard the young woman say, 'Who was *that*?'

'No one we need bother about,' said Freddy. Was she imagining things, or was his voice slightly louder? She resisted the urge to bang the door closed and stomped off with her head held high.

*Food*, she thought, scanning the quaint, winding main street for a suitable establishment. She caught sight of a tearoom – Miss Millie's Morsels – and despite her qualms at the twee name, crossed the street to look. *Perhaps not.* The sandwiches on offer consisted of coronation chicken from locally reared free-range hens, honey-roast Hazeby ham, Sage Hazeby cheese, or organic cucumber. 'At that price they ought to be gold-plated,' murmured Jade. If that wasn't enough, the tearoom was full. 'Didn't fancy it anyway,' said Jade, and moved on.

Further down the street, a pub sign swayed gently in the summer breeze. Jade peered at it: *The Duck and*

*Druid. Hmmm, interesting.* But at the top of the menu by the door it said *Your Local Gastropub*, and main courses started at 14.5. Not £14.50: 14.5. *Ugh.* Jade grimaced and kept going.

She passed a gift shop, an old-fashioned sweet shop, a small independent cinema named Reel to Reel showing three films she'd never heard of, a boutique catering for people who liked pastels, and Hazeby Little Theatre, which was bigger than its name would suggest and currently staging *A Midsummer Night's Dream,* with two special open-air productions at Hazeby Stone Circle. 'Ooh,' said Jade, and made a mental note to check that out. *Perhaps my customers will be there. Can't see them anywhere else in this place. Though sometimes the most conventional-looking people are the ones burning candles and casting spells. You never can tell.*

She moved on, and was about to sidestep a small queue when she noticed a sandwich board beside it which said *Bacon or Sausage Roll and Any Hot Drink £5.* Jade paused, then read *Add a Cookie for £1.50.*

*Sold!* She lined up behind two workmen discussing football. 'I'll give up my season ticket if it carries on like this,' one said. 'At this rate we'll be relegated to the Billy No-Mark league, and in my view that's no place for Hazeby Victoria.'

'Monkton United are a good side, though,' said his comrade. 'That new centre forward was a good signing.'

'Why aren't we signing players? Tell me that.'

Jade tuned out and after a small amount of deliberation decided she would prefer a bacon roll. *I wonder what Jack – what Hugo will say when he visits. You'd think I'd be used to his new name by now.* She tried to visualise her son strolling around Hazeby-on-Wyvern. His visits tended to be short, since as well as his computer science degree, he was running some sort of tech business from his Oxford digs. 'Are you sure you should be doing that?' she had asked. 'Won't they stop your bursary?'

'Hardly,' he had replied, with a sickening grin. 'Two of the awards committee have invested a small stake in the business.'

'Oh.' Jade felt rather small, as she often did during conversations with her son. 'In that case, I suppose it's all right.'

'You worry too much, Mummy,' he had replied, giving her a gentle punch on the arm.

'I wish you'd call me Mum, like you used to,' she said. 'Mummy sounds so – so polo club and trust fund.'

*Maybe he will like it here*, she thought, looking across the road to a wine bar called Ritzy's. The queue moved forward, and she went with it.

'What'll it be, love?' said the woman behind the counter. She wore a white apron with *Betsy's* embroidered on the bib in fancy red script.

'Can I have a bacon roll, a cup of tea and a chocolate-chip cookie, please.'

'Coming right up.' The woman yelled 'Bacon tea choc chip!' over her shoulder. 'That'll be six fifty.' Jade reached for her purse. 'Don't think I've seen you before. Are you visiting?'

'No, I've just moved here.' Jade raised her voice slightly. 'I'm opening a new shop, Crystal Dreams. Crystals and candles and healing spells, that sort of thing.'

'Oh, a hippie shop,' said the woman. 'Fair enough. If they want a vegan sausage roll or a falafel wrap, send them here.'

'Will do.' Jade grinned.

A young man brought her order, nicely wrapped in two paper bags, and Jade noted the robust cardboard sleeve on the cup.

'Milk and sugar's on the end,' said the woman. 'Hope to see you again.'

Jade poured a splash of milk in her tea, fitted the lid on, and wandered out of the shop. She had her lunch, but where to eat it? She saw a signpost pointing right which said *TO THE RIVER*.

*Bound to be a bench or two there*, thought Jade. *Who needs a posh riverside café with prices to match?*

She turned right and found herself on a short

24

cobbled street with a slight downward slope. At the end was a walkway, then railings, then a boat. A barge, painted in racing green with its name picked out in gold and red: *Coralie*.

As Jade walked down the road, she noticed a sandwich board propped outside. At the top was a line drawing of a boat sailing on a sea of open books, and underneath: *The Book Barge. Come Inside for Books Old and New.*

'Don't mind if I do,' said Jade, and strolled towards it.

# CHAPTER 4

Normally, Fi and Geraldine worked from twelve to two together in summer.

If it wasn't raining too hard, people took their lunch to eat by the river and were often tempted by the possibility of checking out the books. Geraldine usually had her half-hour lunch break at half past eleven, and Fi, if she didn't skip it, would snatch a snack at about three o'clock.

Today, however, Fi was on her own. Therefore it seemed as if every tourist and townsperson had decided to visit the barge at once. Normally, Fi would have been thrilled, but for the first time in several years she had a sudden, deep longing for a quiet office to herself, a computer and a huge pile of work to complete without needing to talk to anyone. The customers she usually found to be at worst wearying, and at best engaging and funny, today felt more like an infestation.

Several older people from one of the cruise boats had clustered round the table where a celebrity author's latest bestseller was on display. They were discussing it loudly and in one person's case, flicking through to see if it looked as good as the previous one and to check their favourite character hadn't died, while giving a running commentary on his and his wife's opinion of the series. Fi could only hope he would actually buy it, preferably before the pages were bent or the spine broken.

Nerys, a shy young mum from the town, who regularly visited the book barge now her youngest was at school, had slipped into the boat and was currently wedged in the corner with the cookery books. *Oh bother*, thought Fi, *she's after a job. I'd completely forgotten I'd asked her to pop in today.*

She signalled that she'd be with her as soon as possible, but Nerys frowned and tipped her head sideways.

Before Fi could find out what Nerys was trying to say, she was bombarded by a group of tourists rattling off a series of questions from the sublime to the ridiculous.

*Do you have a book about the history of lampshades? What do you know about the local stone circle? How long did it take to sail from the Netherlands to Hazeby-on-Wyvern? Oh, you're not*

*Dutch? Why aren't you Dutch? It's a Dutch barge. Do you have any DVDs? Books are all very well, but the film's always better. Who's got time to read?*

'Psst.' Nerys had squeezed between two of the wider ladies and was pointing surreptitiously. Near the exit, a middle-aged woman standing by the little selection of books and gifts for babies and toddlers that Geraldine usually supervised appeared to be slipping things in her bag.

'What the—' Fi took a step forward.

A small, bearded elderly man wearing a Panama hat barred her way and pointed with his walking stick at her collection of secondhand travel books. There was a good risk they'd be knocked on the floor at any moment. Some were valuable.

'Do you have *The Light Side of Egypt* by Lance Thackeray? Or maybe *Travels in Tartary* by M Huc? Someone told me you might. He said he saw a copy of at least one of them here last February. Or maybe the February before. Or maybe September.' He smiled brightly and expectantly. 'I can't see either. Or did he mean the book barge in London?'

'Sh-shall I go over to the kids' section?' whispered Nerys. 'If she's doing what it looks like she's doing, maybe she'll stop.'

'Would you?' whispered Fi. 'I'd be so grateful. In fact, if you can help me fend people off for the next half hour, I'll pay you.'

'Don't be silly,' Nerys murmured back. 'You look after your customer.'

'Please, have a seat.' Fi ushered the older man to a leather armchair. 'I'll check in my database.'

'Excel,' said the man, recoiling as she tapped on her tablet, as if Fi was about to dabble in a witch's cauldron. 'I don't get on with that. It's not as romantic as index cards.'

'Do you sell cappuccino?' interrupted a young woman, holding a popular rom-com book. 'I'd like to have a quick read before I decide.'

'Not yet, I'm afraid,' said Fi. 'Hopefully in a week or two. I could—'

'I shan't bother, then.' The woman shrugged, put the book down on a pile of autobiographies and made her way to the exit.

'That was rather rude,' said the old man.

'It happens,' said Fi. She made a quick search. 'I did have a copy of *The Light Side of Egypt*, but I'm afraid it was sold last year. *Travels in Tartary* . . . no, I've never had that. I could try and find you a copy if you fill out a form, including the maximum you'd pay. Some of these old books cost a great deal.' Her records showed that *The Light Side of Egypt* had sold for £50. A good day. She sighed.

'Thank you, dear,' said the man, taking the form and a pen.

Fi gave him a smile, hoping he'd put a nice big

maximum suggestion in the relevant box, and prepared to take payment from a couple with a small handful of books. She glanced at the children's section, where Nerys was tidying in a purposeful manner. The middle-aged woman sidled to the exit, then made a dash up the steps. As she collided with another woman coming down, a small cascade of tiny books and toys slipped from under her jacket, but she didn't stop, pushing at the newcomer to get away. As Fi rushed up and climbed the steps to follow, the thief could be seen running towards town. Pursuit was pointless.

'Blimey,' said the newcomer, rubbing her arm. 'Never heard of a book-lifter before.'

Quite why this statement was annoying Fi wasn't sure, but it was. She wanted to say, 'Excuse me, my books are good enough to steal, I'll have you know,' but that wouldn't be good customer service, so all she said was, 'I suppose stealing books is better than stealing booze. Maybe she's trying to improve herself.'

'With *Miffy Goes To The Zoo* and an eraser in the shape of a dinosaur?' said the stranger, picking up the fallen items. 'Each to their own.'

She was possibly older than Fi, maybe taller than Dylan. As she had descended into the boat, in Doc Martens decorated with patterns and swirls, her knee showed through a slit in a long purple and black skirt.

Above the neckline of a short-sleeved black top, a lovely choker of black beads adorned a slender throat, with two bunches of thick, dark curly hair on either side. Fi, who was wearing jeans and a plain T-shirt, felt suddenly drab.

One of the older tourists bustled over. 'Don't go calling the police. Maybe she has children she can't afford to buy books for.'

'Maybe,' said Fi, doubting it very much. 'There's no point, anyway. By the time anyone catches her the evidence will be gone. It's just a loss.' She closed her eyes for a moment. The items gone were few and not terribly expensive, but that wasn't the point. Maybe she was a soft target. She waited to see if any of the well-oiled river-cruise tourists would offer to pay something to make up for it, but they didn't. She glanced at the secondhand books which the old man had been interested in. It would have been worse if one of those had gone.

The newcomer wandered around, looking at the merchandise, then leaned in close as Fi took the last tourists' payments and wrapped their books. 'Was that a local?'

'What?'

'The shoplifter. Was she local? Do you get a lot of that sort of thing? It's a bit rubbish.'

'I didn't recognise her,' said Fi. Who was this woman? Was she always this direct? She imagined the stranger in a board meeting at the company where Fi had worked, talking to the managing director in that way, telling him he was a fool, that his projections were wrong, that he'd chosen the wrong partners. He'd have bitten her head off. But Fi imagined this woman wouldn't care. In fact, she'd bite him back.

Remembering how much she'd loathed the man, Fi decided it was a cheering thought. 'Sorry, that wasn't very helpful. These sorts of things happen everywhere, I guess, but Hazeby-on-Wyvern is generally calm and pleasant. Are you staying here and worried it's a den of crime? If so, you needn't.'

'I've just moved in,' said the woman. She put out a hand. 'I'm Jade Fitch.'

'Fi Booker. I was a newcomer four years ago. The locals can seem distant to start with but they're friendly once they get to know you. Welcome.'

'Thanks. Are you into the supernatural? You've got a selection of books on magic and ghosts and standing stones and so on.'

Fi tried not to pull a face indicating precisely how much she *wasn't* into the supernatural. 'Not really, but plenty of locals are. There are all sorts of local legends and it's good business to have the books to go with them. I try to keep an open mind.'

'I've finished, my dear,' said the old man, thrusting his completed form into her hand. She'd entirely forgotten about him.

'Thank you, sir,' she said. 'I'll get back to you as soon as I can.'

'I see that you have a copy of *More Magic* by Professor Hoffmann,' he said. 'Such a lovely cover, isn't it? I'd be tempted, but I'm lucky enough to have a copy. It was my grandfather's. Published in 1890, dear,' he informed Jade. 'Rather wonderful – Victorian conjuring tricks and so on. Anyway, I'll bid you adieu.' He tipped his hat and left.

Jade looked where the old man had pointed. 'It is nice,' she said. 'Why's it in prison?'

Because of its value, Fi had put the book on a high shelf with a little bar across it and a card marked *Please do not touch. Please ask if you want to know more about me.*

'It's delicate.'

'Ah,' said Jade. 'Anyway, pleased to meet you, Fi. Sorry for all the questions, but I'm opening a shop in town called Crystal Dreams on Wednesday.'

'Oh! I've heard about it,' said Fi.

Jade's face darkened. 'Who from?'

'A friend. He thought your display was wonderful.'

'Not Freddy Stoat?'

'I think you mean Stott, and no, not him.'

'Are you sure it's Stott?' Jade stared blandly, but the corner of her mouth twitched. 'Stoat seems far more apt.'

# CHAPTER 5

Jade roamed around her shop, straightening a geode, rehanging a necklace, adjusting the pyramids of incense sticks. How could the morning go so slowly?

She looked at the window of the shop, on which she had written in laborious glass marker *GRAND OPENING – NOON TODAY!!!* The clock on the wall said it was five past ten. It had been delivered the day before, an impulse buy. The minute hand was the handle of a broomstick, the hour hand the pointed hat of a revolving witch, with *Time Flies* instead of a maker's name. It wasn't particularly easy to tell the time by it, but Jade suspected someone would probably snap it up anyway.

She picked up her phone and typed a message to Hugo: *New shop opens in two hours!* She added a photo of the shop front and pressed *Send*, then watched the phone confirm sending and delivery. *No use waiting for a reply*, she thought. *He's probably in a lecture, or a class, or whatever you call them. Or doing something I wouldn't understand.* She put the phone on the counter and resumed drifting round the shop.

She was rearranging the miniature cauldrons in height order when the phone buzzed and she nearly dropped one. She set it back on the shelf carefully, then fetched her phone.

*Looks great, Mummy!* She winced. *Just one thing – your window needs a central focal point. Sides are great, bit blah in the middle.*

Jade frowned, then typed: *You're an expert with computers, not shop windows.*

The reply came two minutes later. *I'm not, but I showed Spud and he agrees. His mum is a retail consultant and window stylist. She wrote a book about it. Want me to gift you an e-copy? I can do it now.*

Jade gritted her teeth. *I'll manage.* Spud, if he resembled Hugo's other friends, probably drove round Oxford in an old Jag that had been the family's Sunday runabout and had a knack for spotting designer goods in charity shops. She wandered outside, took a deep breath, and faced the window. What she saw made her heart sink gently, like a soufflé that had peaked too early. 'He's got a point,' she muttered. *Say thanks to Spud for me*, she typed.

The reply came at once. *Will do. Good luck, Mummy! XXX*

Jade grimaced at the phone, then put it in her pocket and resumed gazing at the window. *It isn't terrible. It's far from terrible.* She remembered a time, years ago, when she had had to put big signs in her shop window to hide the fact that she couldn't afford the stock for a decent display. Or the awful run-up to Christmas one year, when she had had to buy wrapping paper from the pound shop and wrap empty boxes to fill the space. Or the time when she had had to sell personal items to cover the rent, watching strangers paw at her CDs and turn up their noses. *Things are much better now.* Yet still that nagging voice in her head. *It isn't as good as it could be, though.*

'What can I do?' she murmured. What would make a splash? She eyed the two geodes, but lovely as they were, they weren't large enough to make the sort of impact she wanted. For a moment, Jade wished she was the sort of arty person who could create a life-size papier-mâché witch. Then she reflected that not even a squad of crack Blue Peter presenters would have been able to knock one up in two hours – no, an hour and three quarters.

*What I need is some magic*, she thought, then spread her hands wide. Of course! That lovely book she had seen in the book barge a couple of days ago.

*No way*, she told herself sternly. *I bet it's expensive. You're already into your overdraft and you haven't opened the shop yet.*

*But it would draw people in. You could put it on a plinth in the middle of the window and shine spotlights on it. That book deserves to be showcased.* Maybe the owner – Fi, was it? – would be willing to do a deal. Jade remembered how she had seemed rushed off her feet, though she wondered how well the book barge did. The most goods she had seen moving out of the shop had been under the jacket of that thief.

*I could say I was doing her a favour*, she thought, and her brown eyes glittered. She went back into the shop, got her bag, locked up, and set off.

*Play it cool*, she told herself, and slowed her pace to a stroll. *I doubt anyone will get in first.* Then she stopped dead. *How much is it worth?* She pulled out her phone and did a quick search, then whistled. *Could be an investment.*

She started walking again, taking slow, deep breaths and practising a nonchalant expression. It was all she could do not to rub her hands. Inside, she was doing a little jig of excitement.

The road that led to the barge was quiet. Jade hoped that meant the shop would be, too. *Better conditions to negotiate.* She paused at the gangplank, drew herself up and marched along it, then had to duck anyway to get through the door.

The shop was even more empty than she'd hoped, since nobody seemed to be in. Jade's fingers twitched as she walked quietly around it, trying to remember where she had seen the book. That elderly man had mentioned it, and he had been standing – that was it. The book was on the top shelf, facing out, protected only by the bar across it. Jade's hand moved towards it, then she pulled her arm sharply back. *You're better than that, Jade Fitch. Anyway, there might be CCTV.* She moved away from the shelf and yelled 'Shop!'

Fi hurried through the door at the rear, smoothing her hair. 'Sorry, I was just putting things straight. Oh, hello.'

'Isn't it risky to leave the shop unattended?' said Jade. 'Especially with shoplifters about.'

Fi's eyebrows drew together slightly. 'That isn't a regular occurrence.'

'How would you know?'

Fi walked to the shop counter and tapped the tablet. 'I do keep track of my stock.'

'I'm sure you do.' Jade began to wander, inspecting the shelves.

'Were you looking for anything in particular?'

Jade, with her back to Fi, did a tiny shrug. 'Not sure... Just browsing.'

'Hang on, isn't it your grand opening today? I'd have thought you'd be busy in the shop.'

'Everything's in hand.' Jade moved to the Occult

and Supernatural section, picked up a large palmistry book, inspected the cover and replaced it. If the price wasn't right on her main target, perhaps that would do at a pinch. 'Oh yes, that magic book. The one that chap was talking about. How much was it again?'

Fi tapped on her tablet. 'A hundred and fifty pounds.'

'Isn't that a bit overpriced?' Jade kept strolling. *Play it cool . . . play it cool...*

Fi snorted. 'It's a first edition, in great condition. I could sell it to a collector for more than that.'

'But will you? I mean, that old boy liked it, but he already had a copy.' Fair play to the woman, she seemed to know what she was doing. But there could still be a deal to be done.

Jade moved into general non-fiction and pulled out Aldous Huxley's *The Doors of Perception*. She turned it over and read the blurb. *Maybe if I put in a lower offer...* 'How does ninety sound?'

Fi laughed. 'Low.'

'A hundred, then.'

Fi shook her head. 'I'm sorry, but it's still a no.'

Jade sighed. 'Never mind. Hope you find a buyer.' She put *The Doors of Perception* back and moved to the opposite corner of the shop, where she studied the spines of the sports section. *Stay calm, make her wait, get her twitchy . . . then she'll jump at it.*

Behind her, someone entered the shop. *Darn, now*

*I'll have to wait for them to go.* She pulled out a book about the history of Newmarket racecourse and opened it at random.

'Hello again,' said Fi, in a tone which suggested she knew the person. 'Anything I can help you with?'

'Just thought I'd have another look-see. You know me.'

Jade froze. *Isn't that...* She turned slightly, still looking at the book, and out of the corner of her eye, she saw him.

Freddy Stott, making straight for the Occult and Supernatural shelves.

Jade managed not to scream 'No!' She wanted to rush past him and stand in front of the shelf with the magic book, batting him away if she had to. *This is my deal! Don't ruin it for me!*

But it was as if Freddy knew her thoughts and was determined to thwart them. He stood there, hands on hips, so that she couldn't get to the book without elbowing him out of the way. He scanned the shelf, then slowly, so slowly, extended a nicotine-stained finger and extracted the book.

'How much?' he asked, and Jade's heart, which until then had been bobbing gently in an atmosphere of optimism and good humour, plummeted into her Doc Marten boots.

# CHAPTER 6

The start of Fi's day was often quiet. Locals were busy on school runs or going to work or getting their shopping done early. The first big river-cruise boat didn't dock till eleven. The private river-boat people who were moored nearby ate breakfast on their decks, lifting mugs of coffee in river-community solidarity. The tourers might check *Coralie* out later; the local live-aboards were more likely to come round in the evening to share a bottle of wine.

Things usually got going after ten and that suited Fi, who was not a morning person.

But today, around nine thirty, a couple who'd been staying in the town on a short break had arrived early to visit the book barge before they returned home. They had come three times during the previous week, mooching about and cooing over old books and maps. Fi must have interacted with them just the right amount on their visits, because here they were spending proper money on a box full of books. She hadn't been pushy and she hadn't been indifferent. Finally, it had paid off.

Since they were the only customers that early in the morning, and so nice, she made them tea and toast and took pictures on their phone of them sitting on the garden chairs placed on *Coralie*'s deck, with the river winding and sparkling and nosy swans gliding up in hope of crumbs.

Then it went quiet, hopefully to pick up as it usually did mid-morning. Stuart was right: if Fi kept calm and focused, things would work out as she wanted. And she needed to take more breaks.

Fi had recognised that her sense of building panic on the day of the shoplifting was more to do with exhaustion than the rush of customers, or even the theft. Shoplifting was unusual. The only time she'd suspected it before was when a tiny Victorian poetry book with a red cover had vanished shortly after she started up. It wasn't especially rare but bright and dainty: the sort of thing a curious child might pick up and put down elsewhere. There had been a very similar item, priced much higher, in Yesteryear Antiquities a few weeks later. More than once, Fi had wondered about that.

Still, that was in the past. For now, she'd hired Nerys to cover weekday lunchtimes, and today Fi was looking forward to the grand opening of Crystal Dreams. She'd dressed in a pair of wide-legged summer trousers and a pretty top, and wore the earrings with stacks of books on that Dylan had given her. When the morning stayed quiet, she sat on the deck of *Coralie* in the sun, drinking coffee and working on her website, until, as if summoned by her earlier memory, Freddy Stott appeared. Ignoring her, he stomped into the boat.

She followed to find him standing by the older books, wearing his habitual tweed jacket and navy cravat despite the heat. Today's trousers were a murky shade of mustard, his shirt an inedible salmon. He knew a good deal about antiquarian books, and though Freddy complained at town meetings that her shop wasn't bricks and mortar more often than he visited the barge, he did occasionally come to prod the older books and argue over their value.

In fact, he'd bought *The Light Side of Egypt*. It had taken all her nerve not to be beaten down too far on price. He'd then put the book in his wretched shop window, with some swirl-patterned brass items allegedly from 1920s Egypt but more likely from 1960s Habitat, and attached a price tag of double what he'd paid.

Before she could speak, Freddy snatched *More Magic* from behind its bar. He licked his fingers, checked the index, then began to flick through the pages.

'Excuse me, Freddy!' said Fi, putting her hand out for the book. 'There's a sign – you should have asked. Please stop treating it so roughly. You, of all people, should respect an old book.'

Freddy paused in his flicking. 'What are you asking?'

'A hundred and fifty.'

He snorted. 'You expect someone to pay that much in this place?'

'Why not?'

'I'm the only one who would.' He rustled the pages again then turned away. 'Do you mind? I'm reading.'

'Yes, I do mind,' said Fi. 'If you want to buy it, it's one hundred and fifty pounds, please.'

Freddy bit his lip, muttered under his breath, then slammed the book into her hands. 'Don't let it go.'

'I'll do as I please with my own stock, Freddy.'

'Huh.' He stormed up the steps.

Wondering what he was up to this time, and glad the book wasn't small enough to be slipped in a pocket, Fi put the book back carefully and went on deck. After watching Freddy disappear up the lane, she took her time finishing her coffee, then went to her office to stow the laptop and get more stock.

Naturally, that was when a customer arrived, and when Fi emerged into the shop part of the boat, she was surprised to find it was Jade Fitch.

She was clearly trying to look like a browser, but Fi recognised someone on the hunt, and waited. After a while, Jade asked the price of *More Magic*.

*Two people in one day?* thought Fi. *How bizarre.* She told Jade the same price as she'd told Freddy. She had researched the book's worth carefully, priced it fairly and hoped to make a tidy profit. She wouldn't back down far.

'It's a first edition, in great condition,' said Fi, when Jade expressed surprise. 'I could sell it to a collector for more than that.' In fact, doing exactly that was on her business plan: sourcing valuable books and providing a special service for antiquarian book collectors. But she was hesitant. She'd have to think about locked cabinets and better security, but then the book barge might lose the cosy, relaxed atmosphere which contrasted so well with her one local independent competitor: the gloomy, unwelcoming Olde Wyvern Booke Shoppe.

Jade's brain almost churned audibly and they proceeded to haggle, but Jade's best offer was too low for Fi to accept. Jade then proceeded to wander further along the shelves to investigate the sports section. Fi could be wrong, but Jade didn't have the air of a sports fan.

Why was she so interested in the book? It didn't seem particularly occult but it was beautiful, with that lovely Victorian cover with the magician on it. Maybe Jade was a book lover and wanted it for herself. Fi was about to follow her and ask when someone descended into the shop.

It was Freddy Stoat again – no, no – Stott. Fi's mouth twitched as she corrected in her mind the name Jade had given him. It was as well that the town's shopkeepers were on first-name terms.

He greeted her properly this time, with a yellow-toothed crocodile smile capable of curdling milk. 'Just thought I'd have another look-see. You know me.'

*Mmm*, thought Fi. *I do. Why are you back so soon?*

Freddy made a beeline for the book. 'I'll be straight with you,' he said, the smile vanishing. 'Do you recall my Aladdin's Cave window last year? I'm doing something similar: a *tasteful* display to remind passers-by of the magical past. Vases for snakes to be charmed from, ancient lamps, Victorian kid gloves and antique canes, draped in vintage silk shawls in *subtle* colours.'

Jade was now watching with a mildly murderous expression.

Fi smiled. 'How kind of you to support the opening of Crystal Dreams with a complementary display, Freddy.' She tried not to let the smile become a smirk as Freddy's face went puce.

'It – it— Have you seen it?' he spluttered. 'It's a

monstrosity! Purple and stars and . . . and... I shall be having words with the council, and...' He sucked in his breath and let his shoulders relax. '*I* am demonstrating a good display, when a shop owner has taste.'

'I saw Crystal Dreams when I went for a run first thing,' said Fi calmly, 'and I thought it very nice. It's a good deal more subtle than a couple of the souvenir shops, but they're nice too. I like a bit of colour. We don't want people to think the town's full of dreary, old-fashioned, pompous people living in the past, do we, Freddy?'

'Humph. Anyway, I need to finish the display. I have a mannequin in a lovely dinner suit, with cane and top hat, playing a Victorian magician. And I heard that you had the perfect book, which is why I came. I would have come before, but you know how it goes... *Some* of us are busy busy.' He leafed through the pages of *More Magic* once more, his fingers awkward, then shoved it under his arm and fished in his pocket, extracting a roll of banknotes. 'How much for cash? A little deal between traders. No need for the taxman to be involved.' He winked.

'One hundred and fifty pounds,' said Fi. 'And it goes through the books.'

Freddy growled, but she could hear Jade growl too. Of course – Crystal Dreams's window display! When Fi had run by that morning, it was clear that Jade's window lacked a focal point. *More Magic* would look wonderful there. Infinitely better than in Freddy's shop window, with its moth-eaten old clothes and dubious antiques. If only Jade had explained, Fi could have offered to lend it for the opening in exchange for mutual advertising, if they couldn't agree a price.

'Ridiculous!' scoffed Freddy. 'I've seen it online for twenty pounds.'

'I've seen them online for a thousand,' said Fi. 'I had this valued and priced it accordingly.'

'Seventy.'

'No.'

'My dear girl, you don't know what you're talking about.' Freddy forced his face into another crocodile smile and patted Fi's arm. 'You need an expert to explain it to you.'

'I'm not a girl, I'm not your dear, and I've had an expert explain. She was very clear.'

'She? Huh. Antiques is a man's job. Seventy-five.'

'No.'

'A hundred and ten,' called Jade, stepping out of the bow section into the main shop as a young man and woman Fi didn't recognise came in. They had the relaxed look of tourists or day-trippers.

'You?' exclaimed Freddy. 'I didn't know *you* were here.'

'Evidently, given what you said about my shop,' said Jade.

'I'm happy to say it to your face. It's tasteless, *you're* tasteless. The town is going to the dogs. How could you afford a hundred and ten pounds? I've seen the tat in your shop – cheap stuff you probably bought for fifty pounds from bankrupt stock. And why would *you* want a book?'

'For my *interesting* window display.'

'Huh,' said Freddy. 'If you ever get any customers, are you sure they can read?'

'It's important to know how to read when you're casting a curse,' snapped Jade.

The tourists hovered on the steps, looking at each other, then at the scene. The man raised his phone.

'Hello!' said Fi, brightly. 'Welcome to the book barge. These two are, er, doing publicity for Crystal Dreams, a new magic shop in town. It's a kind of fun rap battle between old and new minus the actual, um, rap. Do visit, it's opening today. It's got a lovely display which will include a beautiful old book about magic.' She turned to Jade and murmured, 'A hundred and ten. You've got a deal.'

'What?' Freddy spluttered.

'You're being abysmally rude to Jade,' whispered Fi, 'and patronising to me. I'm not having it. Now please go, I have customers.'

Veins popped out on Freddy's red face. 'She's made a fool of you,' he snapped at Jade. 'That book's worth less than the mass-produced crystal ball in your window. You'd have been better off spending your money on an outfit that didn't make you look like mutton dressed as lamb.' He licked his yellow fingers and flicked through the pages more frantically.

Fi stepped forward, debating how to take the book from him without damaging it more than he was already doing.

'See!' he exclaimed. 'Foxing, mould, a bent page, loose stitching! It's not worth using as kindling.'

'None of that is true,' said Fi. 'Please stop putting your wet fingers on the pages and give me the book.'

The tourist was definitely filming now.

'I—' Freddy licked a finger and turned the page, but his voice was hoarse and his fingers trembling. The book slipped in his hands. 'I—' He crumpled to the floor.

Fi instinctively caught the book and dropped to his side. 'What's wrong? Freddy, what's wrong?'

Freddy's face was going blue. He half reached for her, then convulsed, his mouth half open, his eyes staring in terror. He convulsed once more. Then he fell still.

# CHAPTER 7

Jade inched towards Freddy's motionless body. 'He isn't – he can't be—'

Freddy's spine arched backwards and Jade jumped. She looked at Fi, eyes wide. 'What's happening? Is it a heart attack?'

'It could be,' said the male tourist. 'You two were having a right old argument.'

'He started it,' Jade said, without thinking, then realised that wasn't really an appropriate thing to say. 'Someone ought to call 999. You.' She pointed at him. 'You've got a phone in your hand. I hope you stopped filming when he fell over.'

'Go on, Ben.' His companion nudged him. 'It's a matter of life and death.'

He held Jade's gaze. 'Yes,' he said, unlocking his phone. 'It is.'

Fi knelt beside Freddy and put an ear to his mouth.

'He's still breathing. I'll check for a pulse.' She caught one of Freddy's jerking arms and held his wrist.

'Signal's not great,' said Ben. 'I'll step outside. Don't worry, I'm not leaving.'

'Shouldn't someone be doing CPR?' Jade asked Fi.

'If it isn't a heart attack, I might do more harm than good,' Fi replied. 'He's got a pulse, but it's very fast. His heart must be racing, but at least it's still beating. Freddy, can you hear me? Give me a sign if you can.'

Freddy showed no acknowledgement of Fi's request. His teeth chattered, his head jerked, and he twisted as if he was being electrocuted. He seemed to be in a private hell of his own. *I'm sorry*, thought Jade. *Don't let it be something I did. Even if he did start it. And all for a stupid book—* The book lay forgotten a few feet away, and Jade reached for it. But as soon as she touched it, she withdrew her hand and rubbed her fingers on her skirt. 'Fi... You don't think that book had anything to do with it, do you?'

'What?' Fi stared up at her, her face incredulous. 'Don't be silly. I know it's a magic book, but it's not as if a spell jumped out at him, is it?'

'That's not what I mean,' said Jade. 'He was handling that book and licking his finger to turn the pages, then this happened.'

They both eyed the book.

Fi got up. 'I'll wash my hands. Can you two stay and watch him, please.' She looked at Jade. 'When I come back, you need to wash yours. You handled the book too.'

'Hardly at all,' said Jade. She examined her hands, then clasped them behind her back as Fi disappeared through a doorway. 'I'm sorry, Freddy,' she said, though it had no effect on him. 'I hope you'll be OK.'

'I'm sure he will,' said the female tourist. She smiled at Jade, but stayed where she was. *She's worried she'll be contaminated*, thought Jade.

A heavy footstep signalled Ben's return. 'The ambulance is on its way,' he said. 'Bit of luck – there's one stationed at a fun day in Mistleby, so they should arrive in fifteen to twenty minutes. The police'll be here even quicker.'

Jade gaped at him. 'You called the police?'

'Well, yeah. I mean, it could be a heart attack, or something else.'

'You don't know that,' said Jade.

'Weren't you just saying that the book might have something to do with it?' The female tourist stepped forward. 'That's why the book lady's gone to wash her hands. Maybe it's poisoned.'

'Oh, come off it,' said Jade.

'It could be. Like in that film with the monks. I saw that one Sunday afternoon and it creeped me out.'

'*The Name of the Rose*?' said Fi, re-entering the

shop. 'Oh, um, yes.' She glanced at the book and bit her lip. 'I haven't seen the film, but I've read the book.' She crouched beside Freddy. 'Any change?'

'I don't think so,' said Jade.

'I didn't know it was a book too,' said Ben. 'Who's it by?'

'Umberto Eco,' said Fi, checking Freddy's pulse again. 'It's about the same.'

'Hopefully that means he isn't getting worse,' said the female tourist. 'Ben, what are you doing?'

'Looking for the book,' said Ben. 'Oh, here it is.'

'Ben, don't touch it!' shouted his companion. 'You don't want what he's got, do you?'

Ben took a step back. 'Good point,' he said, giving Fi a wary look. 'I'll order it off Amazon. Anyway, we ought to be getting on.'

'You can't leave,' said Fi. 'The police will probably want to talk to you.'

'If you've got paper and a pen, I'll leave my name and number,' said Ben. 'I'm sure they'll be ever so interested in that video I took.' He gave Jade a sidelong glance.

'There's a pad and pen on the counter,' said Fi. 'Jade, go and wash your hands. Through that door, bathroom is second on the left. Probably best not to use the towel. Don't flush the loo roll, put it in the bin.'

Jade considered saluting, but obeyed.

She had expected the living space beyond the door to be bare and functional, like her flat, and was surprised to find that the kitchen-diner space she entered had pretty turquoise walls hung with retro travel posters. The bathroom was small, but the white suite was up to date and the walls half panelled with periwinkle tongue-and-groove. A selection of shells and seaglass sat in a bowl by the washstand, and the towels matched the walls. Jade washed her hands thoroughly: palms, backs, under nails, fingertips, the span between thumb and forefinger. She reached for a towel, but remembered Fi's instruction just in time. *Quilted loo roll, very nice. She must be making more from this than I thought.*

When she returned, the two tourists had gone. 'How is Freddy?'

Fi shrugged. 'Much the same.'

There was a sharp rap at the door, followed by the entrance of a police officer. 'I've received a report of an incident.'

'Yes,' said Fi, rising. 'This man collapsed suddenly and went into convulsions. We don't know if it's a heart attack, or—'

'The call handler said it was reported as possible foul play,' said the officer. 'Excuse me a moment.' He stuck his head out of the door and called 'Yes, here.'

He returned, followed by a fair-haired, middle-aged man dressed in a grey suit who reminded Jade rather of Daniel Craig. 'I'm Inspector Falconer,' he said. 'I'd shake hands, but in the circumstances… This is Sergeant Blake.' He crouched next to Freddy. 'I assume an ambulance is on its way.'

'Yes,' said Fi. 'Ben – the person who rang – said it would be about a quarter of an hour, and that was a while ago.'

'Not bad,' said the inspector. He took Freddy's pulse. 'Mmm. I'm not a medic, but this doesn't look like a heart attack. To be honest, I'm not sure what it does look like. He's quite cold, isn't he? Maybe get him a blanket. It can't hurt, and he'll be more comfortable.'

'I'll go,' said Fi.

'I take it you're the owner of this boat, then. Obviously I'll have to take some details and a statement.' He paused as the wail of an ambulance siren penetrated the boat, growing steadily louder.

They heard a knock, then a paramedic entered the boat. 'We received a report of a collapse, cause unknown,' she said.

'It might be poison,' Jade blurted. As she said it, she could feel her face flushing.

'Poison?' said the sergeant.

'Cause unknown,' repeated the paramedic. 'But given the way he's moving… He isn't epileptic, is he?'

A great wave of relief washed over Jade. *Please let*

*this be a fit. A mild fit that looks worse than it is. I'll even let him have the book—*

'Not as far as I know,' said Fi.

The paramedic focused on her. 'So you know him?'

'Yes, he's a local antiques dealer. Freddy Stott. He was flicking through that book when it happened.' She pointed to *More Magic.*

'Right,' said the paramedic. 'I'll get my colleague and the stretcher and take him to hospital. We'll take the book, too, just in case.'

'Make sure you wear gloves,' said Inspector Falconer.

'Don't worry, we'll be careful.'

'I meant because of fingerprints. But that, too.'

The paramedic grimaced. 'Thanks for your concern.' She got up. 'Back in a minute.'

'I don't suppose you know this man's next of kin,' said the inspector, taking out a notebook.

'Yes, he's married,' said Fi.

'Her name's Wendy,' put in Jade, and Fi gave her an enquiring look. 'He mentioned her when he was being rude about my shop.'

'I see,' said the inspector. 'Do you know where he lives?'

'Poplar Road,' said Fi. 'I couldn't tell you the number, though. He's the owner of Yesteryear Antiquities on the high street.'

The paramedic returned, accompanied. 'Would you happen to have a carrier bag?' she asked Fi. 'For the book.'

'I've got paper bags,' said Fi, fetching one. 'I'll get my rubber gloves and put it in the bag for you.' Jade watched her slide the book into the bag then tape it up as if it was a perfectly normal thing to do. *How can she be so calm?* Her own heart was thumping in her chest. *When the police watch that video—* She glanced at the counter. The notepad sat forgotten. Could she take it without anyone noticing? Maybe, when the paramedics left, she could—

*No*, she told herself. *You've done nothing wrong. He started it, and the video will show that. You're innocent. No one will blame you.*

*Oh yes they will.*

'Are you OK?' Jade came to to find Fi gazing at her with a concerned expression.

'Yeah, fine,' she said, managing a weak smile. 'It's probably shock.'

The paramedics finished securing Freddy to the stretcher. 'One, two, three, lift.' It tipped to the left as Freddy thrashed about. 'We'll keep you informed, Inspector.'

'Thanks.' They watched the paramedics' halting progress, ending in a sort of three-point turn to manoeuvre Freddy out of the door. Jade imagined them wobbling along the gangplank and crossed her fingers.

Inspector Falconer faced them again. 'So, let's talk. Oh yes, where's the person who reported it?'

'I'm afraid they left,' said Fi. 'The man – Ben – wrote his contact details on my notepad.' She pointed, and Jade made a little huffing sound. She looked at the others to see if they had noticed. If so, they gave no sign, and she relaxed. 'He actually videoed the argument.' Jade did her best not to give Fi a death stare. 'I don't know if he got all of it—'

'There was an argument?' The inspector studied them both, and Jade didn't like the apparent neutrality of his expression one bit. 'I think we should continue this conversation outside.'

'I can't.' The words were out of Jade's mouth before she could stop herself.

'Excuse me?' said Sergeant Blake. He seemed amused.

'I'm – I'm opening my shop at noon. The grand opening.' She looked at her watch. 'I ought to be there now, getting ready. The only reason I came here is because I was thinking of getting a book for the window display.'

The police officers exchanged glances, then turned back to her. 'Which shop would this be?' said the inspector.

'Crystal Dreams, on the high street.'

'Oh yes, I've seen that,' said Sergeant Blake. 'My

teenager fancies that. She's into paranormal stuff. Witches and vampires and that.'

'Witches and vampires, eh?' The inspector raised an eyebrow at her. 'And judging by that book, magic.'

'Um, yes.' Jade swallowed. 'I really should go.'

'If you leave us your details, you may,' said the inspector. 'Name, address, phone number, mobile number. We'll be in touch for a statement.'

'Yes, s— Yes, Inspector. Thank you.' Jade scrawled her contact details on the notepad, then made for the door. The boat seemed to be moving, though of course it couldn't be.

'Good luck with your opening,' called Fi.

Jade raised a hand in acknowledgement. She couldn't speak, her jaw was clenched so tight. She concentrated on getting out of the boat without falling over her feet, then rushed across the gangplank.

She hurried up the cobbled street, stumbling every so often, staring straight ahead of her. She wanted nothing more than to go up to the flat, lock the door behind her, and curl into a ball under the bedclothes. Or better still, fetch her passport, go straight to the train station, and run away where no one could find her. Inside her head, two voices competed to be loudest, one saying, *You've got nothing to be afraid of*, the other insisting, *They'll pin it on you somehow.*

# CHAPTER 8

Inspector Falconer watched Jade depart, his face impassive, then scanned the interior of the shop. Finally, he turned to Fi. 'You'd better shut up shop. I'd ask you to make me a cuppa in the galley while we chat, but maybe not, under the circumstances.'

'I beg your pardon?'

'If there was poison, it could be elsewhere in the boat, too.'

'There's no poison.'

'Then why did Ms Fitch say there was?'

'I've no idea.'

'It's for your safety as well as mine.'

Nerys popped her head through the doorway. Her first shift and the shop was about to shut. 'It's true, then?' she said. 'I heard that that Freddy Stott had a funny turn here after a punch-up. Thought there'd be more mess.'

Of course, it would be all over town in five minutes, with Ben and pal quite possibly telling everyone they met.

'He had a turn, yes,' said Fi. 'But there wasn't a punch-up and he's still alive and kicking.' She winced at the words, recalling Freddy's frantic convulsions, and hoped the inspector wouldn't think she was being flippant when her aim was to reassure Nerys and knock any other rumours on the head. 'All the same, I'll have to close the shop for a bit. I'll pay you for today's hour anyway. We'll try again tomorrow.'

'It is what it is,' said Nerys. She shivered a little. 'I'm glad he didn't . . . you know . . . here.' She waved a hand at the bookshop. 'I mean, obviously I'm glad he hasn't . . . um . . . you know . . . anywhere, but it would have been spooky.' Nerys forced a smile. 'See you tomorrow, Fi.' She withdrew.

'Part-time help?' asked the inspector.

'Today was supposed to be her first day,' said Fi. 'Look, we can sit on the deck if you want to ask me questions.'

'Sounds good to me. Bring whatever you keep your records on. I'll send Sergeant Blake to get takeaway coffees. Or would you prefer tea?'

'Coffee, please. Betsy's is nearest and cheapest.'

'What type of coffee?'

'The only choices are black or white and an oat milk option. Black for me. No sugar.'

'You heard the lady, Blake.'

Inspector Falconer sat beside her at the little table on the deck like a friend. Around them, the busy, happy noises of a river and riverbank in summertime mocked the image of Freddy contorting on the floor of Fi's shop. She looked at her watch, then sat on her hands to keep from twisting them.

'Had you wanted to go to Ms Fitch's grand opening?' said the inspector.

'Why not?' said Fi.

'Know her well?' asked Inspector Falconer.

'No. She's new to the town. Been here a week, I think. She popped in the other day, but that's it.'

'Fair enough. Now, can you tell me what happened? Take your time. I can see you're distressed.'

*Can you?* thought Fi, her gut wrenching as the image of Freddy flailing drifted through her mind. *I'm trying to seem calm. Is that the right thing to do? But screaming in panic isn't good, either. I feel . . . shocked. What's happened in my shop?* She kept her eyes on the inspector's face. It was a nice face, his fair hair greying at the temples, his blue eyes apparently friendly. He was about her age. The kind of man she'd look twice at in normal circumstances. However, these weren't normal circumstances.

She described Jade's arrival, followed by Freddy's return, the argument, her agreeing to sell the book to

Jade, then Ben and his companion turning up. It was pointless to pretend the row hadn't happened. 'Freddy was flicking through the book, when he first came and again later. He licked his fingers as he looked. Then he collapsed. It h-happened s-so f-fast... One minute he was standing there shouting, then on the floor in such pain... I thought he was having a h-heart attack. I-I thought h-he was going to...' Fi's voice rose in panic. She closed her eyes, took a deep breath and opened them.

The inspector made a squiggle in his notebook, then glanced up. 'Here comes Blake with the coffee. Take a good gulp, Ms Booker, and he's brought cookies too. Have one. It'll help. Then we'll go over things in more detail.'

Fi did as she was told. She felt cold despite the sun.

'Right, then,' said Inspector Falconer, 'let's save some time. How much of that argument was filmed?'

Fi thought back. 'Possibly from the moment I offered the book to Jade.'

'How much did this Ben hear beforehand?'

Fi revisited the scene in her mind. Probably he'd heard her tell Freddy he was rude and patronising, and before that . . . hadn't Freddy suggested Jade's customers couldn't read, and hadn't Jade mentioned a curse? Fi could feel her face flame. It was just a turn of phrase, but who knew what the police would squeeze out of it. If Ben hadn't heard, it need never come to light. 'I don't know.'

'Something's worrying you,' said the inspector. 'Better out than in. I won't twist it.'

Fi took another mouthful of coffee. 'I called Freddy rude and patronising. Which he is. Anyone in the town will say he's not popular.'

'Why?'

'He underpays and overcharges. He takes things beyond a fair profit. He hints his stuff is too good for the average townsperson, though half of it isn't even antique, but he smarms over anyone he thinks is posh or rich.'

'Any whisperings of anything worse? Selling stolen goods, that sort of thing?'

Fi remembered the Victorian verse. She'd priced it at three pounds, a profit of one pound on what she'd paid. Freddy had sold a book that looked identical for twenty pounds shortly after it went missing. But . . . she had no proof. 'Not that I've heard.' She relaxed a little.

'OK, so the locals – including you – aren't that keen on him, but it was Ms Fitch he was arguing with, and she's been in the town five minutes from what you say. What was so wonderful about the book that they had a heated argument over it?'

'Oh, but it wasn't about the book.'

The inspector leaned forward. 'What, then?'

Fi swallowed another mouthful of coffee. 'Freddy's a bit of a snob. There's already a split in the town: modernising things versus keeping them preserved in pseudo olde-worlde aspic. Freddy's shop is next door to Jade's. He doesn't like what she sells and he doesn't like her window display. He says it's tasteless. It's not, it's just different. His has probably been the same for fifty years.'

'They had a sparring match over a window display?' The inspector looked incredulous.

'Freddy started it. And it wasn't about the display, more the whole concept of Crystal Dreams.'

'Which is?'

'Hippy mumbo-jumbo, I assume.'

'Not a fan?'

'No, but the town needs variety and as Sergeant Blake said, the teenagers will be thrilled.'

'Gotta love a teenager,' said the inspector, with the sort of grimace that suggested parenthood. 'Did Ms Fitch give as good as she got?'

'Well, yes.' There was no point pretending. It would be in Ben's witness statement. 'It was annoying. The book barge is usually a calm place and I like it that way. I wished they'd take it outside and maybe push each other in the river.' The words were out before she could stop them.

The inspector raised his eyebrows. 'My pen stopped working for the last sentence. Now for the book itself. How much were you selling it for?'

'A hundred and fifty pounds.'

Inspector Falconer's eyebrows became almost stratospheric. 'And you had it on an open shelf, with every man and his dog wandering around?'

'This is a bookshop,' said Fi. 'People visit if they're interested in books and a high proportion are looking for bargains. Not many seek antiquarian items and so far, I've only kept a few. I was thinking I might branch out… The point is, it's not the sort of business to attract shoplifters. Generally. Anyway, *More Magic* was on a high shelf with a guard in front to stop it falling and a sign saying "*Please do not touch. Please ask if you want to know more about me*". Me being the book. What's its value got to do with anything?'

'Who said it had?' The inspector began writing again. 'People who knew its value might want it for their own. But if Ms Fitch is right and it was poisoned, you and your customers have been at risk ever since you acquired it.'

'It's nonsense. She's probably remembered that arsenic-green book in the news a while ago.'

The inspector turned the page. 'Last questions, then I'll leave you in peace. When did you get it? Where from? And how long has it been on display?'

Under his scrutiny, the more Fi tried to remember, the more her mind felt blank. 'It's only been on the shelf a few days. Three? I'll be honest, I can't recall where I sourced it from. I might not have. My Monday assistant sometimes finds things and gets half the sale. Occasionally people leave books outside, as if I'm a charity shop. I usually give them to Oxfam, but occasionally I keep a book if it looks special. Bear with me and I'll see.'

Fi typed her pass number into her tablet and opened the stock file. She filtered the stock records and frowned. *More Magic* wasn't there. Panicking, she filtered by the word 'magic' and found it listed as *Magic, More*. She rolled her eyes. It was a Geraldine data-entry special. Under source, it said 'antique'. That could mean found in a shop, sold by someone doing a house clearance, or pretty much anything. Purchase price was blank, which was what Geraldine did when she bought things, because she never spent more than fifty pence.

Fi remembered *More Magic* lying in a pile Geraldine had set aside for her to price up. She'd adored the book's cover and felt a frisson of what she'd hoped was anticipated good luck. How wrong could you be. She'd searched online and realised its potential value depended on its interior, so she'd checked a few pages at random before sending photographs to an expert. Then she'd marked it with a fair price. If it hadn't sold by the end of the summer, she'd have sold it online.

Geraldine's data entry was so vague that Fi

normally went through and corrected things, but she hadn't had time recently. If she admitted that, it would make her look incompetent. She'd have to get the details from Geraldine and update her records later.

'My Monday assistant Geraldine made the entry after I priced it,' she said. 'I can't recall sourcing it, which means she did. Normally we make sure the records are straight at the end of the day, but she was going on a retreat that evening and left early, and we agreed we'd do it when she returned. I remember the book in a pile and I remember researching its price, but I can't recall if she said where it was from, or even if I asked, and I haven't thought about it since. It's been a busy few days and I honestly didn't expect there to be much interest, let alone two people haggling over it the same morning.'

She fell silent and the inspector waited for a while, then closed his notebook. 'Thank you, Ms Booker. I'll come back soon and find out what you've unearthed while digging.' He looked past her. 'Here comes the SOCO team.'

'Scene of crime officers?' said Fi, following his gaze to two approaching police officers, carrying cases. At the end of the gangplank they paused to acknowledge her and the inspector, then put protective covers on their shoes. 'But no crime's been committed! This is my business! My *home*! My son will be home from school in a couple of hours. You can't—'

'I think you'll find I can,' said the inspector. 'And what's more, I'm going to.'

# CHAPTER 9

'Thank you very much,' said Jade, as a woman wearing perhaps one more scarf than strictly necessary, especially in June, held her card to the machine. *Beep!* 'Would you like a bag?'

'Oh no, that's fine.' The woman slipped a copy of *Manifest Your Destiny* and a ylang-ylang candle into her fringed bag.

'See you again, I hope,' said Jade, as the woman worked her way through the waiting people to the door.

A young woman stepped forward with a small bottle of sandalwood essential oil and a silver cat charm. 'An excellent choice,' said Jade. 'Cash, card, or phone?' As she rang up the purchase on her card reader – she had wanted a proper old brass till, but the prices had nearly made her faint – Jade silently congratulated herself. Somehow, she had got things right for once.

She had arrived at the shop at a quarter to twelve to find five or six people waiting outside. 'Almost time!' she said, unlocking the door. 'Don't worry, I will let you in.' A man stepped forward. 'At noon,' she added, opening the door part way and slipping inside, then re-locking it, just in case. She longed to lean against it, like people in TV dramas, and gather her thoughts, but what would her potential customers think? 'Tea,' she said, still rather breathless, and went into the back room to make some.

She had bought a special mug for use in the shop: black, with glittery purple writing on it which said *Witches Do It With Style* in elaborate script. The sight of it cheered her. Not that she had anything in mind for the grand opening beyond switching on the fairy lights and opening the door. *Should I make a speech?* she thought, as the kettle cranked into life. *Do I cut a ribbon?*

*A ribbon...* In the corner was a pile of boxes full of discarded wrapping and things she had used to dress the shop. She dived into it, tossing polystyrene beads and cellophane on the floor, and found a roll of black ribbon which she had used to hang up various items. Rushing back to the door, she threaded the ribbon under the cable which led to the light switch, left a generous allowance, then took it round the door handle and tied it in a big droopy bow. *Hope it works.*

*It's only symbolic, anyway.* She found the shop scissors and cut the loose end. *I'll be able to reuse it afterwards.* She flicked on the fairy lights as she returned to the kitchen, and her arrival there was celebrated by the ping of the kettle.

'Perfect,' she said, and made tea. She added two sugars, in case of shock, and a biscuit on the side. She already had a cheese sandwich in the fridge for lunch, and an emergency banana, but you couldn't be too careful.

Halfway down her cup of tea, a cackle from the witch clock signalled noon. Jade finished her biscuit, then carried the mug to the counter and took a final swig. *Here we go. Showtime!* She picked up her scissors and marched to the door. Her last thought before opening it was *I hope they're still there.* She crossed her fingers and opened the door.

Behind the ribbon were perhaps ten or twelve people. *Gosh. You should do a speech.* Suddenly her mouth was dry. *Come on: you may never get the chance to do this again.*

'Er, hello everyone. I'm Jade, and welcome to my shop, Crystal Dreams. Come inside for . . . magic and mystery!'

No one moved. *Well, come on*, thought Jade, then realised the ribbon was blocking the way. She held her scissors aloft like Excalibur. 'I declare Crystal Dreams officially' – she snipped the ribbon – 'open!'

A small ripple of applause followed, with the flash of a camera, and she fought the urge to bow. 'Do come in.' She stood aside and one by one the customers trickled in.

Jade put on a CD of panpipe music and retreated to the counter, where she had a good view of everything going on in the shop. People wandered about, picking up this and that and talking to their companions. She waited for them to put things down and leave, but no one did. In fact, people began to come to the counter with purchases. She could scarcely believe it. A few asked if she had this book, or that book, and she replied that she could order it, which seemed to satisfy them. 'Let me take your name and number,' she said, and opened the black journal with silver stars that she had put on the counter in a spirit of optimism.

'Will you be offering any workshops?' asked an earnest man in beige trousers and a pale-blue shirt, not at all the customer she had envisaged.

'That depends,' she replied. 'What would you be looking for?'

'Reiki, perhaps. And do you have any Hopi ear candles?'

'I usually do,' she lied, 'but my usual stockist has run out. Can I take your name, and I'll let you know when they come in.'

'Do you do palm readings?' asked a young woman

with student-red hair and a swishy tiered skirt that jingled when she moved.

'I'm considering it,' said Jade. 'If there's enough interest, perhaps I could offer an evening session. Could I take your name and number, please?' She turned over another page in the notebook, hoping she'd be able to make sense of it once the shop was closed.

The clock witch cackled again after what seemed like no time. Jade thought with affection of the cheese sandwich sitting in the fridge. *It'll quieten down in a minute. Most of these people are probably on their lunch hour.*

But more people came to replace them, and more. 'Nice to see something different in town' they said, and 'I'll tell my niece about this place when she visits next weekend' and 'Will you be getting in Christmas stock?'

The witch cackled once more at two o'clock, with an answering rumble from Jade's stomach. That biscuit had been a very long time ago. Jade considered asking the queue to wait while she fetched her lunch, then dismissed the idea. Chomping on a cheese sandwich might break the spell, and shatter her mysterious and possibly magical persona.

When the door opened yet again Jade glanced towards it, curious to see whether the new customer would be the sort of person she expected or not. So far, it had been about a fifty-fifty split. But as soon as she saw the grey suit, the fair hair and the calm demeanour, her courage and confidence trickled away.

Inspector Falconer came straight to the counter. 'Is this a bad time?' he asked. 'I thought I'd wait until your grand opening was over, but you seem quite busy.'

'I am,' said Jade.

'In that case, I can wait. Or I could come back when you've closed.'

'That would be—' Jade broke off as she saw that almost every eye in the shop was on the inspector. She noted the emptying shelves, the gaps in the displays, the haphazard remaining stock. Then her stomach lurched, and she couldn't tell whether it was from fear or hunger. 'Actually, no.' She clapped her hands for attention. 'I'm sorry, everyone, I have an urgent consultation with the inspector, so I'm afraid I'll have to close the shop in a few minutes.'

Inspector Falconer made a noise that, if he hadn't been a senior police officer, she would have called a snort, and she glared at him. 'If you have purchases, can you come to the till, please. The shop will reopen later today. My apologies.'

Eyes wide, people walked to the till and lined up. Others hovered nearby, saying 'How long will it take? Will it be more than an hour?'

'I'll do my best to reopen by quarter past three,'

said Jade. *Too right I will. That gives me time to put out more stock and tidy up before school finishes.*

A few minutes later, she wrote a hasty note on a paper bag and taped it to the shop door: *TEMPORARILY CLOSED DUE TO EMERGENCY CONSULTATION.* 'Would you like a drink?' she asked Inspector Falconer. 'And would you mind if I ate my sandwich? I'm starving.'

'Go ahead with your sandwich,' said the inspector. 'No thank you to the drink. I've just had one.'

*Or you're worried about being poisoned*, thought Jade. 'Shall we go through to the back? I've got some folding chairs, though they're not very comfortable. We could go up to my flat, but it won't be tidy.'

'I'm sure the back room will be fine,' said Inspector Falconer. 'Looks like you've got a promising business, Ms Fitch.'

'It does,' said Jade. 'Certainly if today is anything to go by. Although that could be new-shop excitement. It's whether any of them come back.'

'They seemed keen. Lead the way, Ms Fitch, and let's get this over with.'

Jade placed an extra chair, made herself tea, again with two sugars, and they sat together at the small table. Jade unwrapped her sandwich and took a big bite. 'Sorry,' she said, as soon as she could speak. 'I didn't think it would be so busy. I've only had a biscuit since breakfast.'

Inspector Falconer brought out a notebook and opened it to a fresh page, then took out a pen. *A Parker*, thought Jade. *Not a standard one, either. Must be on a good salary. Or it's a present from someone. I wonder who?*

'Before we begin,' said the inspector, 'this isn't a formal statement. However, I shall take notes and, depending on how the case progresses, I may return for a formal statement. To save time, I'll also tell you that I have spoken to the man who was present when Freddy Stott collapsed and took a video with his phone, and I have watched the footage.' His steady gaze added, more eloquently than words, *So there's no point lying to me.*

'I understand, officer,' said Jade. 'I mean, Inspector.'

'Excellent,' said Inspector Falconer. 'Now, can you give me a brief account of your relationship to date with Freddy Stott?'

Thoughts rushed through Jade's head. *What shall I tell him?* Then she remembered the people standing nearby when she and Freddy had met for the first time, and the young girl filing her nails in Freddy's shop, who nevertheless might have a photographic memory. And Fi, from what she had seen, had a distressing habit of blurting out the truth. She eyed the inspector, who sat perfectly calm, his hands on the desk, the nails short, well shaped and clean, and the gleam of a cufflink peeping from his suit jacket. His face showed no emotion whatsoever: no curiosity, no scorn, no anger, and no sympathy. She ranked him as dangerous and not to be underestimated.

'Right, um—'

The inspector's phone rang, a standard tone. 'I'm sorry, I'll have to take this,' he said. 'Do excuse me.' He took his phone from his pocket and retreated into the shop, pulling the door to behind him.

Jade took the opportunity to finish her sandwich and fetch her banana. She was about to bite into it when the inspector returned. His face was still calm, yet it looked different. 'Everything all right at the station?' she asked.

'Not exactly,' said Inspector Falconer. Then Jade realised that his face looked different because now it seemed to have been carved from stone. 'That wasn't the station. It was the hospital.'

Jade felt as if things were rushing towards her very fast. 'Oh,' she said.

'I've just had bad news. Freddy Stott died twenty minutes ago.'

'Oh dear,' said Jade. 'I'm so sorry.'

'Yes,' said the inspector. 'And while the analysis is yet to come back, everything points to poison. So I'm afraid this is now a murder inquiry.'

# CHAPTER 10

Fi cycled a few miles along the towpath, leaving the police to poke around the book barge. In their white protective gear, they made her think of a swarm – no, a squirm of maggots. It was absurd. Poison, indeed. She hoped Jade's grand opening was going well, and felt guilty for not supporting a new venture in town, but the day had soured and she couldn't face the thought of all the people, the sight of Freddy's shop, or dealing with Jade, who'd looked as if she might pass out earlier. One person collapsing per day was enough.

Ignoring Jade and the inspector's ridiculous views on potential poison, Fi had sneaked the sandwiches she'd made for lunch out of the fridge before leaving the barge. She ate them – after a moment's pause, but with no subsequent ill effects – a few miles down river, then cycled home.

Sergeant Blake was waiting on the deck with a cardboard box. A few people were scattered about, but anyone who might have been curious had long since lost interest.

'So *is* my home poison free?' said Fi.

'Thankfully so, madam,' said the sergeant. 'But the inspector's asked for these books to be taken for analysis.' He pointed at the box. 'Here are some gloves if you want to check it. And here's a receipt.'

Fi took the gloves with a small sigh of exasperation and prodded through. The books were late Victorian and Edwardian, hardback, with covers tooled or patterned in elegant art nouveau swirls or bright pictures of men being valiant and women beautiful. None were valuable but they looked pretty and sold well. She always hoped they'd be read and not turned into display items. 'I've had most of these since May,' she said. 'They've been handled by several people, none of whom have collapsed in front of me. Mark my words, Freddy had an underlying, undiagnosed condition.'

'All the same, Ms Booker.'

Fi rolled her eyes and took the receipt. 'Go on then. I hope to get them back by the weekend.'

She watched him depart, returned her bicycle to the store, and descended into the shop, hugging herself. Everything looked as it should, but felt odd – all those prying fingers, seeking what wasn't there.

The marks on the wooden floor might have been there for days, or they might be from Freddy's scrabbling feet. Were a few specks of white on a shelf dust, pollen or fingerprint powder?

Fi pulled herself together and went outside to put the 'open' sign prominently by the gangplank, then went below to dust and sweep while she waited for customers. This evening, she and Dylan would reorganise the shop and try to exorcise the whole sorry incident.

*Dylan*, she thought, as a customer descended. *Perhaps I should give him the heads-up before he finds out another way.* She greeted the customer and unlocked her phone, then remembered the school had a strict 'no mobiles on in class' policy which Dylan had broken enough times to be on a final warning. All she could do was send him a message on the assumption that he'd read it as soon as the last bell went.

*Before you hear it from someone else: Freddy Stott (antique guy) was taken ill on barge earlier. Emergency services came but all well. Nothing to worry about.*

She grinned at herself. The only thing he'd worry about was her using punctuation.

Dylan arrived home just as she had finished dealing with a customer. She recognised the sound of his bike being flung on the deck, then his feet clattering down the steps.

'Mum! Mum! Is it true?' He waved his phone at her.

'Why would I be messaging lies?'

'Not you,' he said. 'Everyone else. Old Stotty tried to wreck the place and there was a scrap with the crystal-ball lady and Stotty had a fit and the police came in hazmat suits.' He gazed round with disappointment. 'It all looks the same to me. Oh, are you OK, Mum? He wasn't scrapping with *you,* was he?'

'Thanks for your concern.'

'Nana says you'd look after yourself.'

'Nana?' Fi went cold. Dylan's father's mother lived over fifty miles away. 'How does Nana know?'

'She messaged to say she was thinking about Dad and you were probably busy. I told her what had happened.'

'Oh, drat.' Fi checked her phone. A reminder had been set for eleven thirty: *G – 12 – Message the Bookers*. It was the twelfth anniversary of Gavin's death. She always sent a message of condolence to his parents, but today... She started to type, then paused. '*What* did you tell her, exactly?'

'That the old china bloke gave you grief in the boat, then had a stroke, and you've been dealing with the fuzz all day.'

'In those words?'

'There were more emojis but I think she got the drift.'

'Did you say you were sorry about your dad too?'

Dylan squirmed. 'Yeah, but... I don't even remember him. And you never talk about him. Only Nana does. I'm not a kid, Mum. Nana goes on like he was God but I worked out ages ago that Dad dumped us both long before he died.' He looked away, his jaw clenched.

*Gavin had certainly dumped me,* thought Fi. *I ought to have talked about it with Dylan a long time ago.* She sent a brief message of apology and condolence to Annie, then put her arm round Dylan's shoulders. The customer had gone and there were no other adolescents to see. He couldn't complain.

He hugged her back briefly, then extracted himself and ruffled her hair. 'So it *was* the crystal-ball lady that old Freddy was beating up, not you?'

'She's called Jade and no one was beating anyone up.' Fi gave Dylan a brief resumé of the events.

He paced the shop, crouching briefly to check for marks, then touching the books the way Fi had, comforting them somehow. A mass of emotion bubbled up – the horror of the morning, the visit from the police, an overwhelming, protective love for her son – and Fi wished he was little enough to pull onto her lap while she had a silent cry. Then the image of his face if she tried it brought her to her senses and she grinned ruefully. 'Anyway, hopefully Freddy is on the mend, Jade's shop sold a million crystal balls, I get my books back and I never see Inspector Falconer again.' *Or at least not in the line of duty*, whispered her subconscious. 'Haven't you got any homework?'

'Homework?' exclaimed Dylan. 'My dear old mum was attacked by a rabid pensioner and you think I can focus on homework? No chance, woman. You'll have to write me a note for school to say I'm too traumatised. Only gaming can calm me now.'

'Yeah, right,' said Fi. 'Go and make me a coffee.'

Her phone vibrated. Not a message but an email from Annie.

*Thank you. I'm glad you were able to remember eventually. I know you pride yourself on being strong and independent, but perhaps you should consider others occasionally. Nigel and I shall never get over Gavin's death. Our only son.*

*Perhaps it's time to say something we've been thinking for a while.*

*We've never been happy about the unconventional life you've imposed on Dylan, and now it appears that your 'wonderful barge' and 'quaint, quiet little town' are not as secure as you led us to believe. Dylan is a bright boy and deserves a better education than a state school in the middle of nowhere. He certainly ought to be somewhere he can't be attacked.*

*What will happen next? An arson attack? An aggravated burglary? Someone trying to sink the boat?*

*We know you rejected our offer four years ago, but Nigel and I hope you have come to realise that in today's world, the best education might be the only thing to ensure Dylan gets a decent job in future. So we're repeating our offer to pay for boarding school. That will help you return to your old career, now that you've hopefully got this whimsical bookshop idea out of your system.*

*Please think about it. In Gavin's memory. For Dylan's sake. For our sake.*


Fi put the phone down and ran her fingers round her temples. *I'm not answering until I've calmed down*, she thought. *How much worse can today get?*

The sound of a footstep made her look up. Inspector Falconer was descending into the boat and closing the door, his face grim. *There's the answer to that question.* 'What's wrong?'

He peered round, taking note of the area with the curtain. 'Have you any customers at the moment?'

'No.'

'Good. I've put your "open" sign face down on the deck. I have bad news: Freddy Stott has died. There appears to be a toxic substance on some of the pages in that book. On the face of it, the cause of death seems to be poisoning. We can't rule out accident, but a deliberate attempt remains possible.'

Fi slumped in her chair. Freddy… She hadn't liked him, but dead? His poor wife Wendy. But why had he picked the barge to be poisoned in? She gazed at the empty space where the book had been. Where had it come from?

'Have you done that digging yet?' said the inspector. 'We need to know how that book came into your possession. Why the sudden flurry of interest in it? Had you advertised it?'

'No, I hadn't got that far. It was a flurry of two people. And no, I haven't done any digging. I need to talk to Geraldine, as I said earlier. She's on holiday, on a retreat.'

'Can't you contact her?'

'It's one of those disconnected-from-the-world sorts of retreats. No phones allowed.'

'Where?'

'Derbyshire, I think. She didn't say more and I didn't ask. All I can do is rack my brain for what she said about the book when I was pricing it.'

'It's urgent, Ms Booker,' said the inspector. 'I don't want to have to apply for a warrant for your records, but I will if necessary.'

'Look.' Fi opened her tablet, pointed at the entry and several similar ones, then explained about Geraldine. 'A warrant won't help. Till I can ask

Geraldine, I'm stuck. Poor Freddy. Poor Wendy.'

'You didn't like him.'

'No, but there are plenty of people I don't like. I don't wish any of them dead. I'll do everything I can. I promise.'

'Thanks. Goodbye.' Inspector Falconer made a note in his book and left without a backward glance.

Dylan sneaked up with a mug of coffee and a glass of juice.

'Oh, Dylan,' she said. 'Did you hear? Poor Freddy.'

'When will the police arrest you?'

Fi nearly spluttered out her coffee. 'Me? Why?'

'*Your* bookshop. *Your* poisoned book. Are you running a criminal enterprise?'

'This is serious, Dylan.'

'I'm being serious. Can I stay with Alfie if you're arrested?' Dylan walked over to the steps and peered outside.

'Yeah, and you can bake me a cake with a file in it and bring it to me in jail.'

'I can only do flapjack,' said Dylan, sitting on the step. 'Seriously. If they do arrest you, don't let them send me to Nana's. I'd rather stay with Gran. Or shall we go on the run? Cast *Coralie*'s moorings and sail away?'

'If the police had canoes they'd be quicker than *Coralie*,' said Fi. 'You may as well get on with your homework. You've got plenty of time before I'm arrested.'

'Yeah, but physics…' Dylan pulled a face as he sloped back to the living quarters. He walked as if he hadn't a care in the world, but Fi could see the tension in his shoulders, and she was aware of her hand gripping the mug handle so hard that she was at risk of breaking it.

She checked her phone, wondering what would happen when Annie heard the truth. She was fifty-odd miles away, but it was bound to be in the news. People never died in the way that Freddy had.

And then there were her own parents, who lived in Normandy. She had to tell them before they spotted it on a UK news page. And either way, what would happen next?

# CHAPTER 11

Jade stared at the gleaming heaps of coins and the little bundle of notes on the counter. *Maybe I should check it, to be sure.*

*You've already counted it twice.*

*Third time lucky.*

*Ridiculous. You know why you're doing this, don't you? To take your mind off you-know-what.*

*What if I am? What's the alternative? Sit and fret all night?* Jade's hand shot out and mixed the coins into a shining, metallic heap. *Oops, better count again.*

Her inner voice sighed. *At least fetch bank bags.*

Jade got up and went to look. She definitely had some stashed away, but hadn't put them to hand in case that was tempting fate. Eventually she found a handful in the corner of a discarded box. *I hope these are enough.* She pulled the black notebook with silver stars towards her, opened it at the back page, and wrote: *Takings – Day 1.*

Her fingers began the ritual. Five . . . ten . . . fifteen . . . twenty pounds. *How many of today's customers will return?* She slid a pile of coins into a bank bag, folded over the flap, and set it aside. *Well, I've got their phone numbers. And I can always return the books I order if they're no-shows, or use them as stock.*

She remembered the door of the shop opening, and opening, and opening, until it opened to reveal Inspector Falconer in his smart grey suit. She winced. 'That was a one-off,' she said aloud.

Or was it? His face when he came back into the room after that call… 'I'm afraid we'll have to make this more official,' he said, and drew a folded piece of paper from his inside jacket pocket. It was a form, official-looking, and Jade's heart did a little flip.

'You aren't arresting me, are you?'

'Not today, certainly. Not unless you're planning to make a full confession right now.'

She stared at him and his mouth twitched at the left corner. 'Don't worry, Ms Fitch. Let's start again. Can you outline your history with Freddy Stott? I understand you haven't been in the town long.'

'I arrived last week,' said Jade.

'Where from?'

'Is that relevant?'

Inspector Falconer considered. 'Not directly. Is there a reason why you don't want to tell me?'

Jade grinned. 'I'm maintaining my mysterious persona, Inspector.' But under that grin her heart was thumping. She hoped he couldn't tell, and feared he probably could.

'I had a shop in Devon,' she said. 'It didn't work out. I don't like talking about my failures.' *For one thing, it would take too long.*

'I see.' Inspector Falconer regarded her coolly. 'So, Freddy Stott.'

'I only met him two days ago,' said Jade. 'I was putting together my window display and he was passing and was rude about the shop.'

'So he started it,' said the inspector.

'Yes, he did,' Jade blurted, then bit her lip as she understood what she had said.

'I won't ask you any leading questions,' said the inspector. 'If you could tell me what happened next in your own words, that would be very helpful. And give me your impression of him.'

'Snob,' Jade said at once. 'The sort of snob who calls other people's goods tat, then sells his own overpriced tat. A snob, a hypocrite, and a sharp businessman.'

'Surely being a good businessman is a positive thing,' said the inspector. As he spoke, his pen moved over the page.

'Not if it involves sharp practice,' said Jade. 'He grabbed that book to convince Fi that it was damaged and she should lower her price. And probably to put me off it, too. Plus he ran both her and me down in front of two customers. The video guy and his friend,' she added, for clarification.

'So your opinion was that he wasn't a particularly nice man,' said the inspector. 'I won't record this.'

'Maybe he's nice to his wife and his pets, if he has any,' said Jade. 'I certainly didn't see that side of him.'

'Can you recall what Freddy did when he entered the book barge?'

'Not exactly. I was in the sports section and I had my back to the door. When I realised who'd come in, I didn't particularly want to turn round. I'm sure you'll understand that.'

'So did he browse generally, then come across the book?'

Jade considered. 'As I said, I had my back to him, but I didn't hear him wandering about. I had the impression he'd gone straight to that section. Occult and supernatural.'

'That's interesting.' The inspector made a note. 'So he might have known the book was there?'

Jade shrugged. 'It's possible. He might have seen it before, then remembered it when he had a use for it. I do that sometimes.' She shuddered inwardly at the idea that she had a similarity to Freddy.

*That probably isn't the only one*, said her disloyal inner voice. *You like a bargain, too. In fact, you were trying to play Fi as well, to get her to drop the price.*

'So when did you reveal yourself?' asked the inspector. 'Or did Freddy spot you?'

'Fi mentioned my shop and he immediately launched into an attack. I suppose I could have stayed quiet and taken it, but I didn't want to. I don't see why I should.' Her chin went up. She felt like banging the table, but she wasn't sure it would stand up to it.

'What did Freddy do when you revealed yourself? Did he back down?'

'If anything, he got worse. That was why we thought it was a heart attack at first. He was working himself up.'

'Presumably the customer was filming him by then. Did that stop him?'

'Not at all,' said Jade. 'I think he's the sort of man who plays up to an audience.' She grimaced. 'Was that sort of man.'

'Right.' Inspector Falconer's gaze flicked to the form and he continued writing. His script was surprisingly legible, for a man. He glanced up. 'I'll pass you the form when I've finished, so that you can read it and, if you're happy, sign to confirm it as a true account. So you don't have to puzzle it out upside down.' His tone had returned to the neutrality she most hated.

*No, disliked. He's too neutral to be hated.*

*I don't hate him, just his manner. He's probably all right in the pub, with a drink.* She eyed his cufflinks: tiny compasses. *Do those work?* His shirt was plain white, but the fabric and the cut showed it wasn't cheap. *No supermarket two-packs for Inspector Falconer.* Then her gaze moved up to his face and she saw that he was studying her.

'Have you finished sizing me up?' He actually smiled, which was a distinct improvement.

Heat travelled up Jade's neck, then her face. 'I'm sorry,' she said. 'It's a shopkeeper thing. Judging what people might buy, and how much they have to spend. It isn't personal.'

Inspector Falconer wrote the date on the form. 'I think that's everything.' He turned it round. 'So if you'll read it, and if you wish sign, I'll be on my way. I must get back to the station.'

Jade read the form. The inspector had written a factual, bald narration of what she had told him. The episode with Freddy on the pavement in front of her shop was described as 'a verbal disagreement relating to the witness's choice of stock and display arrangements.' Even their final encounter on Fi's barge was couched in the same neutral terms.

'It was so much more than that,' she wanted to say. 'He insulted my shop, and me. And Fi, too.' But she suspected the inspector's version was less incriminating. She took the pen and signed where he indicated.

'Could you fill in your details too, please. It's just for the record, and for if we need to contact you again.'

*I hope you don't*, thought Jade. *I'm sure you're nice to animals and you give to charity, but I hope this is the last time I have to see you.*

*Although if he's based in the town...*

'Thank you,' said the inspector, as she pushed the form across the table. 'I'll head off now.' As he stood up, the witch clock cackled and he jumped slightly. Jade failed to stifle an involuntary giggle.

'I'll have to let you out,' she said, following him into the shop.

'Thanks.' He paused on the threshold. 'I hope the rest of your day goes well. I'll be in touch if we need anything further. Good day to you, Ms Fitch.'

'Bye,' said Jade, and closed the door behind him. She regarded the clock. Was it only three? She felt as if a year had passed since the inspector's arrival. *Better reopen, I suppose. I said three fifteen, and I can't disappoint people on my first day.*

*But can you handle it?*

*Guess I'll have to.*

\*\*\*

The afternoon opening had been almost as busy as

96

the initial one, and when Jade finally closed the shop at half past five her feet were aching and her upper back sore from having to stoop at the counter. She rolled her shoulders and a vision of a large glass of white wine sitting on a pub beermat, misty with condensation, slid gently into her mind.

*Cash up first*, she told herself sternly. *Business before pleasure.*

And now she was gazing at more money than she had ever taken in a single day. OK, so she had more stock than she'd ever had before, which helped, but still…

*Could be a flash in the pan.*

*Could be a step on the ladder*, she countered. *Maybe all those other times were false starts, and beyond my control. Heaven knows I've had enough setbacks. So even if this is a flash in the pan, I'll celebrate it.*

*What, on your own? Who are you going to ask? The woman who sold you a bacon roll? Fi at the book barge? I doubt she wants to meet up.*

*I'll get to know people.* Jade imagined putting two firm hands on her inner voice and squashing it back down where it belonged. *I'll FaceTime Hugo. His classes'll be finished.* Before she could change her mind, she dialled him.

He connected on the third ring. 'Mummy!' From what she could see of him he was wearing a blue sweatshirt, which was a relief. *At least I didn't pull him out of a meeting.*

'Is now a good time to talk?'

'Oh yes, but I can't stay on long. I'm having a chat with someone in Boston at six thirty. Not six thirty their time, though, more like lunchtime. Anyway, how did it go? Are you a millionaire yet?'

Jade smiled. 'Not exactly. But I've taken more today in cash than ever before. I haven't checked the card machine yet. I'm waiting for the email to come through later.'

'That's great! Well done!' He turned away for a second and said 'It's Mummy' to someone off camera. 'So, a good day all round.'

'Um, mostly.'

Hugo raised his eyebrows. 'What happened?'

'It's nothing to do with business. At least, I hope not. Someone… Someone died. Not here, but I was there when it happened. We thought it was a heart attack at first, but it wasn't. The police say it's likely to be poison.'

'What? Tell me!'

Jade gave him as short and undramatic an account as she could. She rather wished she had the inspector's form as a prompt.

'So he was handling a book. What sort of book? And what happened to him? Did he fall over and foam at the mouth and clutch his throat, or what?'

'It was a book called *More Magic*. I was interested in it too. And don't be so callous, Hugo. If you must know, he looked stiff, then collapsed and started writhing and arching his back. He didn't die immediately. The inspector got the news about two hours later. Maybe a bit more.'

'Wait right there, Mummy. Don't hang up.' Hugo stood up, revealing that his sweatshirt said *Class of '66* in flowing white script, and walked out of shot. 'Seb, I need you! Medical stuff. No, now. Mummy's in a pickle.'

Jade waited, tapping her fingers on the counter and eyeing the bank bags. *I'm not in a pickle. It was probably an accident. Odd things happen all the time.*

Hugo returned two minutes later and sat down. 'Sorry about that. I was talking to my flatmate. He's a medical student.'

Jade raised her eyebrows. 'Has he done poisons yet?'

'No, but his dad is in forensics. I told him what you said, and he says it sounds like strychnine poisoning.'

'Strychnine? How would that get into a book?'

'I don't know, Mummy, but you must be careful.'

'I am careful! I just gave the inspector the facts. Anyway, how would I get hold of strychnine, smuggle it into a book, then make sure someone handled it? That's well above my pay grade.'

'That's not what I mean, Mummy.' Hugo's voice slowed as if he was explaining to a child. 'Think about it. A magic book, set up to poison someone, and presumably not on display for long. You're new in town and you run a witchcraft and woo-woo shop. What are the odds that you would spot that book, pick it up and look through it? I hate to say it, Mummy, but you need to be really careful. Because that book could have been meant for you.'

# CHAPTER 12

Fi's phone vibrated and fell off the desk, waking her with a start. For the first time in four years, she wondered where she was, and when she remembered, wished she were anywhere else but.

She'd woken in the early hours, re-running the scene with Freddy and Jade over and over in her head. Unable to sleep, she got out of bed. Surely there must be a clue to where the book had come from. She put the light on and went through her files. Nothing. She'd already sent a text to Geraldine in the hope that she'd see it sooner rather than later. But Geraldine, at fifty-five, was a good deal less likely to check her phone when she shouldn't than Dylan was at fourteen.

Fi made an online search of poisoned books. There were plenty to find: from fourteenth century to Victorian, created using compounds including arsenic, their covers often a lurid green. The risk was to librarians and booksellers. None of those books would kill a man who'd simply taken one off the shelf and waved it about: the worst he'd have got from all that finger-licking was a bad stomach a few hours later. It was hopeless. She searched and thought and eventually dropped off, her head on the desk, only to be woken by her phone.

The immediate dread of where she was and what was happening was replaced by a small amount of hope. There were several messages. Were any from Geraldine?

No.

Supportive ones from Stuart, Jen and Carla, the close friends she'd messaged the previous evening. They'd all offered whatever help she needed, though Stuart was away on business and the others on holiday.

One from Annie: *Have seen the news. Dylan should stay with us till everything's blown over. We can take him to some school open days. We'll come tomorrow. You may stay too, of course. Business will be quiet and it might be best to accept defeat.*

One from her mother. *Good grief, Fi! My phone was out of charge and I've just read your message. Are you all right? It's on the news too. Why a book in your place and not that dusty Olde Wyvern Booke Shoppe, run by that equally dusty old bloke? Call when you can. I imagine you'll be rushed off your feet. People are such ghouls.*

Fi rubbed her eyes and, groaning, opened up the news on her phone. Halfway down the page was a small article linked to Wyvernshire news.

*Bizarre unexplained death of shopkeeper in riverside idyll. Antiques dealer Frederick Stott, 67, of picturesque Hazeby-on-Wyvern, died suddenly yesterday after handling an old book bought from a specialist shop. There are local rumours that this was an ancient poisoned book, like those that appear from time to time in antiquarian circles. This may be a tragic accident. However, the police are said to be investigating, which indicates that other possibilities are being considered. No arrests have yet been made, and we are still to receive a reply from Wyvernshire Constabulary.*

A hyperlink led to an article about the arsenic-covered books and Fi ran her hands through her hair in despair. 'It wasn't green!' she muttered. 'And I'm sure arsenic doesn't make you bend into an arch.' That image reminded her of something: tetanus. She did another internet search and the images of people arched in agony looked horribly familiar. But surely Freddy had been vaccinated – and if not, could he have been infected that easily?

Fi was about to do another search when Dylan

103

knocked on the door. 'Mum? Are you OK? It's eight o'clock.'

She shook herself and replied first to her friends, then her mother and mother-in-law.

*Thanks Mum. Please don't worry, Dylan & I are all right. I'll ring later.*

*Thanks Annie, that's very kind, but we're OK & Dylan has exams next week.*

Then she went to face the day.

***

Unsurprisingly, Fi's mother, who had run customer-facing businesses all her life, was right, while Annie, who'd been a secretary to a professor of Classics for most of her career, was wrong.

People were ghouls.

They were queuing up outside the boat by eight-fifteen. The moment Dylan opened the wheelhouse door to get his bike for school, they pushed past him and piled in like invading pirates.

Fi texted Nerys. *I know we said lunchtime, but if you have time after the school run, I'd be glad of the help.*

A pause, then a reply: *Is it safe?*

*Yes. I'll pay extra today as it's so out of the blue.*

A longer pause. *OK. Maybe eleven.*

Some of the customers were people Fi knew from round the town, who greeted her with a cheery smile. The rest were strangers: tourists, perhaps, or people who lived in town but didn't mix.

Whatever group they fell into, they poked and peered like true bibliophiles, touching the older books, pointing and whispering.

A woman who ran one of the hair salons sidled up to Fi and pointed at the floor by the bestsellers. 'Did old Freddy die here?' she whispered.

The room fell silent.

'No,' said Fi. 'He collapsed there. He *died* somewhere else.'

'You poor thing. It must have been awful.' The salon woman opened her slightly bulging eyes very wide while leaning forward, presumably in anticipation of details.

Fi felt as if she was about to be attacked by a pug. 'Yes, it was.'

'Was it *this* kind of book that killed him?' The greengrocer's assistant picked up a 1960s paperback edition of *Appointment With Death.*

'No,' said Fi. She was overwhelmed with the urge to take the book from him or find a pair of gloves. But it was impossible. Someone else was gingerly holding a slightly worn hardback edition of *Dracula.* Another was perusing a red cloth-bound copy of *Dr Jekyll and Mr Hyde.* A woman from the florist's had picked up *Half Magic* from the children's table, using a tissue from their bag. One of the young bartenders from the wine bar was sniffing, actually sniffing, a brand-new edition of *The Poisonwood Bible*.

'I heard he was screaming for his mother,' said the florist.

'I heard he looked like a zombie,' said the salon owner.

'He looked like a zombie anyway,' muttered the bartender. 'He probably poisoned himself. Nasty old goat.'

'True enough,' said the greengrocer's assistant. 'He gave me a fiver for my gran's tea set, saying it was mass-produced silver plate, then put it on sale for a hundred with a label saying it was unique.'

'Shouldn't speak ill of the dead,' said the florist, pursing her lips. 'He bought a lot of flowers from me.'

'Who for?' said the salon owner. Now she resembled a pug who'd found a dish of gravy. '*I* heard that Amy Reilly always has lovely roses. *And* new jewellery all the time.'

'Who from?'

'My lips are sealed.'

'What's Amy Reilly got to do with anything?' said the florist. 'I don't ask people who they're buying flowers for. I'm sure Freddy bought them for Wendy.'

'You know where they go,' said the salon owner. 'If he was buying them for Wendy, why was she complaining that romance had gone long ago?'

'Amy Reilly's got her own husband who dotes on her.'

'Roger Reilly?' snorted the bartender. 'He threatened to do for old Freddy once in the bar. Admittedly, they'd both had a few. Perhaps he'd been swindled over a bit of old tat too.'

'It wasn't tat,' argued the greengrocer's assistant. 'And I never said I wanted him to die.'

'I'd have expected a book like that to be in Mr Darcy's Olde Booke Shoppe.' The florist pronounced it Oldee Bookee Shoppee. 'My dad was taught chemistry by old Mr Darcy back in the sixties, when he was still a teacher. They used to work with mercury and all sorts. Dad says it was fun before health and safety went mad. Did you buy the book from Mr Darcy to sell on?'

Fi swallowed and straightened her spine. She'd worked for a large company for years. She'd addressed board members, investors and representatives from the bank in various tricky situations. A few curious townspeople were nothing to be scared of.

She put on her corporate smile and her presentation voice. 'I gather you've heard about Mr Stott's death and I appreciate your support, as his collapse was horrible to witness. However, I'd like to assure you that the police have checked my remaining stock very carefully and found nothing of concern. Since you're here, I'd be delighted to tell the story of the book barge...' She launched into the speech she'd given more than once to bank managers, explaining the layout, the ethos, the mixture of old treasures and new finds. 'I'm thinking of starting up a book club soon and providing a venue for a writers' group, so I'd be delighted to take the names of anyone who's interested.' The ideas had come into her mind unprompted but her speech seemed to break the spell. People moved about more naturally, a few drifting out of the boat and others collecting books to purchase.

By the time Nerys arrived at ten past eleven, the flow of customers had reduced a little. Fi was conscious that most were locals and felt uneasy. Tourists made up a good deal of her customer base, tempted by the unusual and ready to spend good money.

Nerys put her bag away in the private quarters and looked nervously round. 'Surprised they're not taking pictures.'

'Me too.'

'The cruise boat's been stuck upriver. Engine had gone.'

'Oh, good. I mean, I see.'

'It's just moored. Is the shop really safe?'

'No one's dropped dead yet.'

Nerys stared at her.

'Yes, it's safe,' said Fi. 'Can you take payments while I tidy up? People have been rummaging as if it's a lucky dip.'

Fi left Nerys and made her round of the boat, reorganising and straightening. She kept visualising Inspector Falconer running in and telling her that twenty people had dropped dead after visiting her shop that morning. Telling herself not to be absurd, she moved towards the section in the aft. Two men were muttering behind the curtain, now drawn back, which could make a spare bedroom or games room for Dylan and his friends when the shop wasn't open.

'Course it was a bribe. Otherwise how'd he get the golf-club captaincy?'

'Everyone expected it to be you, Frank, but maybe it wasn't a bribe. Maybe he dropped hints about how it would look.'

'How what would look?'

'MD of a pest-control business over an antiques dealer. Not posh enough. You know how snobby golf clubs are.'

'It's not 1950.'

'Some things never change.'

Someone tapped Fi's arm. 'Do you recommend this?' She was waving one of the bestsellers.

The muttering in the aft section stopped and Fi had to concentrate. Tourists were descending into the boat.

Two hours later, things were slowing down again. It would have been nice if the number of customers had equated to increased sales, but almost everyone was intent on seeing a possible crime scene, taking surreptitious photos and buying something cheap out of guilt.

Nerys left and Fi distracted herself by making notes about a book club and writers' group. She became so engrossed that it wasn't until someone delicately cleared their throat that she glanced up. In front of her stood Wendy Stott.

'Hello, Fi.' The widow was dressed in a black calf-length sleeveless dress. Her eyes were red and her hands clasped a small clutch bag as if she was afraid it would fly away. Round her neck was a plain gold chain.

'Oh, Wendy,' said Fi. 'I'm so sorry. I—' *I'm what*, she thought. *My shock is nothing compared to yours.* Wendy visited the bookshop occasionally and had eclectic tastes. 'I don't know what to say.'

'I'm not blaming you, if that's what you're worried about,' said Wendy. 'It's a tragic accident, I'm sure. Freddy probably had a weak heart. He was that sort of age.'

'I'm sure the police will clear things up quickly. How are you managing? Is there anything I can do?'

'I don't think so. I'll have to sort the shop out, of course, so I'll be quite busy, but otherwise I have my garden to retreat to. Nature is a wonderful thing.'

'Yes.'

Wendy looked around her. 'I just came to remind

110

myself of where my Freddy was when he was last happy.'

'Er…'

'I understand it was rather brief.' Wendy gave her a wan smile. 'But I can't believe that was your fault. Yesterday must have been a terrible day for you, as it was for me. I wanted you to know that you have my sympathy. We'll both get through this, won't we?' She left the boat with dignity.

Fi watched her go and a sob rose in her throat. Would she get through this? Surely, in the end, Wendy would move on, but could the bookshop survive? If people only came through curiosity, thinking they were at risk of imminent death, she wouldn't last the summer.

She put her head in her hands. Maybe she should send Dylan away and work out how to close down without him around.

Someone cleared their throat. It was feminine, not as prissy as Wendy, but hesitant. Fi looked up.

'We need to talk,' said Jade.

# CHAPTER 13

Jade regarded Fi, disgruntled. She had spent the morning serving customers – several of whom had bought lucky charms and amulets – and placing a book order which had required checking her bank balance before pressing the *Buy Now* button. However, in the intervals between those things, she had worried. Not enough to consider wearing a lucky charm herself, but enough to make her twitchy.

Every time a customer addressed her unexpectedly, or replaced an item on the shelf with the slightest noise, she jumped. *I can't go on like this*, she thought, after practising deep slow breathing and visualising someone drawing a box for the umpteenth time. Not even a CD of ocean waves was working. 'Right, I'm closing for lunch at one,' she announced to the shop. 'That gives you five minutes to browse or buy. I'll reopen at two. Probably.'

The customers grumbled under their breath, but shuffled obediently to the till. That done, Jade had taken twenty pounds from her cash box, made a note in the notebook, and set off for the book barge. She had taken the initiative, closed her shop when business was booming, and come to have things out. And now Fi was staring at her as if she had two heads.

'Talk about what?' Fi said.

'You know what.'

Fi sighed. 'I've done nothing else all morning.' She ran her hands through her short brown hair, which made no difference.

'Been busy, then?' Jade surveyed the otherwise deserted barge.

'I have, actually,' said Fi. 'Lots of locals coming to see the scene of the crime. If I was that sort of person, I'd draw a chalk outline on the floor and move the crime section next to it.'

Jade snorted. 'I'd be tempted. I tell you what, Freddy would've done that.'

Fi managed a grim smile. 'If there is an afterlife, he's probably looking down on me and shouting "What are you doing, woman? This is the perfect opportunity to shift those dogeared Agatha Christies!"' She began to laugh then stopped, a guilty expression on her face. 'Oh dear. I'm getting hysterical. This is the first chance I've had today to be – well – normal.'

'I've had a run on charms and amulets,' said Jade. 'I'm thinking of ordering in some rabbits' feet. Fake ones, of course,' she replied to Fi's pained expression. She studied Fi, who had faint purple shadows under her eyes and was dressed in a plain aqua T-shirt and jeans. Jade suspected it was the first outfit that had come to hand that morning. 'You look as if you've got the world on your shoulders.'

Fi slumped on her stool. 'That sounds about right. Keeping this place afloat is precarious at the best of times, but now... Yes, I've got people coming to gawp, but I've sold more 50p bookmarks than anything else this morning. I doubt I've covered my mooring fee.' She gazed around the barge helplessly. 'This is my home. Mine, and my son's. I doubt I could afford a one-bed flat in town.'

'That's why we need to talk,' said Jade. 'I can't be doing with policemen popping in and out and asking questions.'

A straggle-haired backpacker descended carefully into the boat. 'I didn't think you'd be open,' he said.

'Yes, we are,' said Fi. 'The boat's been inspected, and everything's fine.'

He made a noncommittal noise and headed to the science fiction and fantasy section.

'You don't look fine,' said Jade, more quietly. 'You look as bothered as I feel.'

Fi sat up straight, then slumped again. 'Who am I

trying to kid?' she said. 'What with people, my mother-in-law, and my assistant going on a retreat when I most need her—'

'You need a break,' said Jade. She eyed the backpacker, who was watching them. 'In fact, I'm taking you out to lunch. I'm guessing you haven't had lunch, if you've been busy.'

'I have been busy,' said Fi. 'I know it doesn't look like it at the moment, but when the river cruise lands... It tends to be either feast or famine.'

'I can't promise a feast,' said Jade, 'but I'll go as far as a bacon roll and a brew. Or hummus or something,' she added, remembering the rabbit's foot.

'That's very kind but I should treat you, since you're new in town.' Fi addressed the backpacker. 'I'm closing shortly for lunch, so if you want to buy anything...'

The backpacker rolled his eyes and left without a word.

'I hate the silent lurkers,' said Jade. 'Are you vegan, by the way? Will you mind if I eat a bacon roll at you?'

'Not at all, and no I'm not,' Fi replied. 'I don't eat much meat, but I like chicken and fish. We could bring lunch back and eat it on the deck.'

'Excellent.' Jade rubbed her hands. 'Lead the way.'

Fi brought in the sandwich board and locked up, then they ambled slowly up the cobbled path to the high street. 'I thought Betsy's,' she said. 'Is that all right with you?'

'Oh yes. Is the woman on the counter Betsy? I was chatting to her the other day.'

'That's right. She and her husband used to run a restaurant together in the town. When they split up, she opened Betsy's. The restaurant lasted for two months after she'd gone.'

Jade chuckled. 'Sisters doing it for themselves.'

'Absolutely. I used to have a corporate job, which I hated, but it was only when Gavin left that I gave it up and took the plunge with the book barge. Eventually.' She studied Jade. 'How about you?'

'I prefer being my own boss,' said Jade. 'Not that I'm necessarily any good at it.'

'You seem to be doing fine,' said Fi.

'At the moment I'm a novelty, like a talking dog. We'll see how it goes when things settle. But yeah, I don't take well to being told what to do. Apart from a bit of supermarket delivery work in 2020, I've worked for myself almost since I left school.'

In the end, Fi paid for Jade's bacon roll and her chicken salad sandwich, and Jade said she would buy lunch next time. They wandered back to the boat. Now that the river cruiser had gone, it was quiet apart from two teenagers sitting on a bench, sharing a cone of chips and staring at their phones.

For the first time, Jade noticed the two garden

chairs and small table perched at the end of the boat, with a string of bunting hung above and plant pots spilling over with foliage. 'Your boat's lovely,' she said.

Fi gave her a surprised smile. 'Thank you. I've tried to make it as nice as I can. Dylan – my son – would like more space, but we manage. I'll go in and make us drinks. Tea or coffee?'

'Tea, please.'

'Milk? Sugar?'

'Milk and . . . one sugar, please.' She had been about to say two, but best not to let that become a habit. Two bacon rolls in one week was bad enough.

'Make yourself comfortable,' said Fi, and let herself into the boat.

Jade sat carefully in one of the garden chairs, which was more substantial than it looked. She stretched her legs and relaxed. *Maybe one day I'll have a nice outside space. A balcony, or a roof terrace, or maybe even a garden.* She eyed the teenagers, then peered down the river. Was that another boat coming?

Fi came back with two blue and white striped mugs. *I should have been thinking of what to say, not woolgathering*, thought Jade. 'Thanks,' she said, taking the mug Fi held out. 'So, the talking.'

'Would you mind if I started my sandwich first?' said Fi. 'I've been on the go all morning and I'm hungry. I daresay you are, too.' Jade watched her unwrap the sandwich and take a bite, looking into the middle distance as she chewed. *You're not eating like a particularly hungry person. I reckon you're worried about what I'll say.*

She let Fi eat half her sandwich, then could wait no longer. 'I was talking to my son last night on FaceTime.'

Fi swallowed her mouthful. 'Oh yes? Does he live somewhere else, or was he out for the evening?'

'He's at Oxford, doing his degree. I ended up telling him about the murder. As it happens, one of his flatmates is a medical student, and he reckoned it was strychnine poisoning.'

Fi froze, mid-chew. 'Strychnine?' she said, through her sandwich.

'Apparently. No idea where that would come from; surely it would be banned or regulated. That wasn't all.' Fi was leaning forward and gazing at her. 'Hugo said it might not have been meant for Freddy.' She caught the flash of surprise in Fi's eyes when she said her son's name. 'I know. I named him Jack, a nice normal name, but he decided that there were too many Jacks when he was fifteen and renamed himself.'

Fi made an impatient gesture. 'Never mind that. Who did he think the poison was meant for?'

'Me.' Jade sipped her tea, which was rather strong.

118

'Think about it. I'm new in town and I run a witchy, magical sort of shop. What's the betting I'd pick up that book?'

Still watching her, Fi picked up her drink and took a deep draught. 'Or me. I don't know how the book came to my boat, and I won't until Geraldine gets back, but somehow it's here. It's luck that I thought it might be valuable and only turned a few pages when I handled it.' Suddenly, she looked like a child who had had her ice cream stolen. 'I didn't think I had any enemies, but maybe I'm wrong.'

'Hopefully it isn't that,' said Jade. 'You might have rivals who want to put you out of business. Another bookshop, or a business that reckons you're stealing their trade.'

'That's horrible,' Fi murmured, holding her mug as if it was the middle of winter and the mug her one source of warmth.

'*Or* someone's trying to frame one of us.' Jade waved her bacon roll to push home her point. 'That makes more sense. They couldn't know that Freddy would be the first person to handle the book enough to kill him. Maybe they didn't care who died, or even if they were only a bit ill and recovered, so long as the police picked up the crime. Best case scenario, one of us gets convicted, and at worst, it messes with or finishes off one of our businesses.' She eyed Fi, who was regarding her with horror. 'I'll be honest with

119

you. I've had the inspector come to the shop and take a statement, and I have a distinct feeling that I'm a person of interest. Given the circumstances, I suppose I'd have to be.' She made her voice as casual as possible. 'How about you?'

Fi ate two more bites of her sandwich before answering, though Jade suspected she'd stopped enjoying it. 'He's come here, yes,' she said. 'They closed the barge while they went over it, and sent me away, and they've taken a box of books to check. So I'm probably in the same position as you.'

'Which means we should work together.' Jade set her mug down harder than she'd meant and Fi flinched. 'You know the area and the people, and I bet customers gossip in your shop. And I've got – Hugo's a technical wizard, and he knows lots of people like his med-student flatmate. That will help a lot, because neither of us can do internet searches for strychnine or whatnot. They're probably monitoring us right now.'

Fi gazed around her, eyes wide, and Jade searched her mind for what she could bring to the party. 'I notice things,' she said, eventually. 'I read people. That's how I've managed to survive.' She regarded Fi earnestly. 'I don't think you poisoned that book and I know I didn't, so we need to work together and trust each other if we're going to sort out this mess. Otherwise, we're probably screwed.'

She couldn't read Fi's expression, and decided to take a chance. She stuck out her hand. 'Partners?'

Fi gazed at her hand, then her, and with a tiny, decision-made sigh, grasped Jade's hand and shook it. 'Yes. Partners.'

# CHAPTER 19

Fi watched Jade stride into town as if she hadn't a care in the world. A pretty red scarf floated in the breeze, making her look as if she was an indestructible, fiery goddess. If she could make the effort, so could Fi.

She washed up their lunch things in the galley then put on a little make-up, changed from jeans to floral shorts and added turquoise beads for good measure. If Jade was flame, then Fi could be a water goddess. She chuckled at herself in the mirror – either the witchy stuff was catching or she'd lost her marbles. Either way, she felt better: more ready for whatever nonsense the afternoon would bring. Less defeated, more rational.

As she settled back to work, Fi pondered the conversation with Jade over lunch. She hadn't revealed everything about herself, and suspected Jade hadn't either. Why would they? They'd only just met. She sensed Jade was haunted by something, but whatever it was, she respected Jade's desire to keep it private and had no desire to pry. At the same time, however, Jade had shown an astute business mind and Fi was curious about Crystal Dreams. Was it a calling, or an opportunity? Was Jade an uncanny New Ager or a canny entrepreneur? In normal circumstances, Fi could see the two of them working together to benefit each other – bouncing ideas about, not hidebound by local traditions. But not now. First, they had to work out why they'd been caught up in a suspicious death caused by a poisoned book.

Jade had invited her for a meal at six to pool ideas. It was time to come up with some sensible ones.

Fi opened her tablet to make notes, then realised there was a good chance that it would be confiscated by the police for analysis, and they'd be able to dig up anything she'd deleted. Jottings of ideas, even retrospective, might be misinterpreted. Sometimes, nothing beat paper. She took a small notebook from her bag and stared at it, then looked at the table which displayed miscellaneous items: notebooks, pens, bookmarks. The one in her hand was too small to lay out her thoughts. The pretty ones were good sellers. Ignoring a curious glance from a customer, Fi slit open one of the larger paper bags and laid it flat. She sat for a while, tapping her teeth with her pen, before starting to scribble.

*FS – born & bred. Inherited shop. Not liked by (m)any.*

*Who, specifically?*

She had to be honest and rational.

*Me – irritated, patronised, possibly stolen from. Little other contact except:*

*Mayor's Christmas Do for local businesses – publicly treated as newcomer by him and doubts cast on my business as too hippy.*

*Public town council meetings – opposing sides on modernisation/decoration*

*Worth murdering for? No.*

She tapped her teeth again. Jade would have to do the same for herself.

Who else?

As Fi was thinking, Mrs Brummell, an elderly lady who was a regular customer, ambled up with a book displaying a discreet image and sentimental title. It was the latest steamy romance from a bestselling author. A young man nearby looked on in horror. Fi suppressed a smile. Mrs Brummell devoured that genre. She just didn't see why she couldn't do so wearing sensible shoes.

'I hope you're all right, dear,' said Mrs Brummell. 'It'll blow over. Today's news is tomorrow's chip paper.'

'Unfortunately, you can't make chip paper out of

the internet,' said Fi.

'True,' said Mrs Brummell. 'The townspeople will lose interest, mark my words. I daresay the local rag is thinking up a nice obituary. That'll be a work of fiction. Let's be honest, Freddy Stott wasn't popular. I'm not sure he had any friends apart from poor Wendy, presumably. The paper will have to interview her if they want anything positive to report. Anyway, how much is this book, dear? And perhaps you could order the next one in for me.'

Of course, the townspeople.

Fi's mind churned as she jotted a couple of names, then folded up the paper bag and put it in her pocket. She served Mrs Brummell then the anxious young man, who bought a book on mushroom identification. As the shop went quiet, she made a cup of coffee and scanned her own bookshelves for anything that could help. Realistically, with all the true crime books and biographies of murderers, how could she find what she sought? Her fingers itched to do an internet search but it was too risky. The paper with her notes on crinkled in her pocket and she returned to her serving area to search the news on her phone. Little had changed, but Stuart had sent her a message:

*Just back and still willing to help. Sorry, I don't know where Geraldine's retreat is. Is it important? Are things so bad that you want to join her? I can work from the barge and serve your customers too for an hour or so if you need a break. Chin up. XXX.*

'Knock knock!' Kevin, who ran the town ghost tour, was standing at the top of the stairs.

'Hi. What's up?'

Kevin descended into the shop then fixed his gaze on Fi. 'I was thinking about including the boat on my tour. I could bring the punters to experience the vibes of Freddy's last moments. Too soon?'

'Too soon.'

'Really?'

'I'm having a hard enough time getting paying customers in as it is. Come on. I support you, even though you've never seen your own ghosts—'

'Harsh.'

'But true. Please don't make things worse for me.'

'OK,' said Kevin, with a shrug. 'It was worth a try.'

Fi watched him leave through narrowed eyes. She knew without a doubt that he'd bring the tour as close to the boat as he dared.

Dylan was late home from school because he'd gone to Crystal Dreams with his mates.

'What's it like?'

'Really cool,' said Dylan. 'Half the kids from school were there. Us boys know it's nonsense – although if she adds a D&D section that'll be awesome – but she'll never get rid of the girls. They love that sort of stuff. Here.' He opened a bag. 'I got you something.'

He produced a small globe and flicked a switch in the base. It rotated, projecting the constellation of Sagittarius on the ceiling in soft, blue, spinning light.

'Er…'

'I know you're an Aquarius,' said Dylan. 'Or at least, I worked it out. But you don't believe it anyway and the Sagittarius pattern's better. I thought it would be nice in your cabin. If you can't sleep, you can watch it.'

Fi gave him a hug. 'Thanks. What did you get yourself?'

'Chloe said I should get crystals for protection.' Dylan rolled his eyes. 'I bought some candies in the shape of runes. Want one? The X is *super* tangy.'

'No, thanks.'

'Alfie asked me and Max over to have tea and play on the Switch. I said I wasn't sure I could leave you on your own. Even with a magic Sagittarius globe and tangy runes.' He looked worried. 'If you'll be OK, can I go? We'll do some revision, I promise.'

'No, you won't,' said Fi, 'but actually that's perfect. I'm going out, too. We'll leave together just before six and you can meet me outside the Swan at eight and walk me home. Deal?'

'Deal.' Dylan paused. 'I asked them to come here

127

and usually they would, but…'

'I know,' said Fi, giving him another hug. 'It'll all be over soon.'

*** 

At six, Fi was in the alley behind the shops in the high street, deducing which gate led to Jade's backyard. As with many old buildings in town, the impressiveness of the facade was in stark contrast to the rear. Jade's place was no exception. A minuscule square of uneven paving led to a dark, narrow, mossy passage, and thence to a back door.

Fi made her way along, feeling rather illicit and hoping this really was the best approach. People rarely came down the alleys except to make deliveries, so no one could remark on the fact that two strangers who had nothing in common but Freddy's collapse were meeting up like old friends. On the other hand, if anyone did notice her it would look even odder than using the front door.

Jade ushered her in. 'Sorry, the gardener's on holiday.'

'Don't beat yourself up,' said Fi. 'You've just got here, and those spaces are tricky with so little light.'

'I've made a chicken spinach pizza couscous casserole.'

'That sounds, er, intriguing.'

'I had to work with what I had,' said Jade. 'And I've got a whiteboard upstairs so we can do – is it blue-sky thinking?'

'Yup.'

'Want a tour?'

'Yes, please,' said Fi. 'My son was in earlier and he was really impressed. Though I'm afraid he only bought sweets and a little globe thingy.'

'I'd love to say I recognised the resemblance but there were a lot of teenagers.'

Jade took Fi round the shop. The layout wound in a logical path round displays: knick-knacks, serious-looking kits, decorations, books, trinkets and little things like sweets that had big mark-ups. As far as Fi could tell it had something for everyone, from the unbeliever seeking a pretty ornament to the dedicated practitioner of a wide variety of beliefs ancient and modern. It was calm, and reflected the same atmosphere of intimate welcome that Fi hoped she provided at the book barge.

'It's lovely.'

Jade grimaced. 'You probably won't say the same about upstairs, but dinner's ready and hopefully edible.'

The flat upstairs was predictably full of half-emptied packing crates. There were few personal touches, as if Jade had put all her time into the shop so far. On the mantelpiece was a photograph of a tall, slim young man with shortish dark hair, presumably Hugo.

'So, where do you get strychnine?' said Jade.

'The only thing I remember is a book where a dog ate strychnine rat poison and they fed it mustard to make it throw up,' said Fi. 'I might have remembered that completely wrong. But I keep thinking that if I'd realised, I could have fed Freddy mustard… Does it work like that, though?'

Jade opened her laptop. 'Let's find out.'

'No!' Fi slammed the laptop shut, nearly trapping Jade's fingers. 'Not that way. If the police seize your laptop they'll find your search.'

'Not if I'm incognito. Not if I delete the search.'

'They still could. It's not worth the risk.'

Jade rolled her eyes. 'All right. Let's eat and blue-sky think.'

They took bowlfuls of the casserole into the sitting room. The food looked an unholy mess, and Fi felt slightly ashamed that she was reluctant to try it. But after Jade had eaten a few mouthfuls and survived, Fi discovered it was a delicious mixture of chicken and spinach in a rich tomato sauce. As they ate, they took it in turns to write on the whiteboard. Fi copied what she'd written about herself earlier and Jade added her own involvement. Then they crossed both through.

'There are rumours that Freddy bought flowers and jewellery for Amy Reilly,' said Fi.

'Who's she?'

'I only know her by sight, but I know her husband

Roger better from the civic events. He runs the last independent chemist's in town.'

'Is he a qualified chemist himself?' Jade's pen was poised.

'I don't know. He might just own the shop and hire people.'

'But if his wife was rumoured to be cheating on him, he probably doesn't like Freddy.'

'Apparently Roger and Freddy were on the verge of a fight in the wine bar not long ago.'

'Right.'

'Then there's Mr Darcy,' said Fi. 'He doesn't approve of me.'

'Mr Darcy? Love interest?'

'Very much not. About eighty. Sells old books, but apparently he used to be a science teacher at high school a long while ago.'

'Old books. Science. Right. Anyone else?'

Fi bit her lip. 'I heard something else. What was it… That's it! Golf.'

'What's golf got to do with anything?'

'The presidency, captaincy, whatever it is, of the golf club. I've been to the occasional social there. A couple of dinner dances with… A friend, a while ago.'

Jade raised her eyebrows. 'You don't strike me as the ballgown type.'

'You'd be surprised,' said Fi. 'It sounded like

Freddy got to be whatever it is when someone else was expected to get it, but they're in pest control and it didn't have the right snob value.'

'Who's this pest controller?'

'The name I overheard was Frank. It can't be that hard to find out his surname. This is a small place.'

'Anything else?'

'Not that I can think of.'

They stared at the whiteboard. It could be anyone or no one.

But it was a start.

# CHAPTER 15

Jade regarded herself in the mirror. Plain, mid-length black skirt – check. Sensible blouse (usually kept for official appointments) – check. Low-heeled court shoes (ditto) – check. Hair tied back – check. She longed to add a scarf or a string of beads, but no. She was on a mission.

The night before, once Fi had gone, she had ruminated as she washed the dishes.

Writing on a whiteboard was all very well, but what could they actually do? *We've both got businesses to run, and if Fi's right about not using the internet, even incognito…* She scoured a bowl viciously and put it upside down to dry. *Fi's got time during the day, because she's got helpers, but she's known. I'm not…*

And so she had resolved to visit Mr Darcy's bookshop the next day. *Apart from anything else, I*

133

*might be able to pick up a bargain. Not that I'll be telling him that.*

She had been good and not Googled the shop, instead using the Yellow Pages which had been left, damp and crinkled, by the door to her flat. Ye Olde Wyvern Booke Shoppe had a premium listing: a box of its own, with a line drawing of a stack of three ornate books. The shop's name was in dark, cramped Gothic script. Underneath: *The home of the discerning book lover.* Jade shuddered. *Best not to be too optimistic about the book bargains.* The address was 54, Market Street, and there was a map. *9 am-5 pm, Monday to Saturday.*

Jade gave her reflection an approving nod and checked her watch. Two minutes to nine. She put her purse, keys and phone in the small black handbag she had fished from the back of the wardrobe. *Don't look too keen. That might make him suspicious.*

She took her phone out of her bag and tracked the progress of her book order. It was still in process. 'People are waiting, you know,' she told it. She closed her browser and considered texting Fi, then remembered she didn't have her number. *Probably as well. No point sneaking around at night then leaving a message trail.* She dropped her phone in her bag, zipped it closed, and set off, using the back door.

Even at a pace which seemed agonisingly slow, she still reached Ye Olde Wyvern Booke Shoppe at five past nine. It was everything she thought it would be. The window was cluttered with books on little Perspex stands. Little folded cards next to them proclaimed *First Edition*, *Collectable* or *Signed Copy*. The books themselves were almost all hardback, often with plain leather covers. A card in the corner of the window said *Valuations Performed: please enquire for further information*. Jade pushed open the door and the bell clanged to proclaim her entrance.

Inside, the shop was very different to Fi's book barge. For one thing, there were far fewer books, and most of them were kept in glass-fronted cases which Jade suspected were locked. In the corner, a small ratty man with fluffy white hair, wearing a greenish tweed jacket, a white shirt and a bottle-green knitted tie watched her beadily.

'Are you seeking something specific?' he asked, before Jade had been in the shop a minute.

'Not really. Just browsing.'

'This isn't a browsing establishment,' he replied, leaning on the counter. 'People who come here tend to know what they want.'

'Ah,' said Jade. 'Do you have an occult and supernatural section?'

'No,' he said, looking as if she had offered him a live frog to eat.

'Pity,' said Jade. She moved to inspect another case.

'So if we don't have what you're looking for, it seems pointless to linger.'

She bristled at his rudeness. 'Are you always like this with customers?' she asked.

'What do you mean?' he snapped. 'I've been running this establishment for fifteen years and no one has ever complained.'

'I'm not complaining,' said Jade, 'just asking.' She decided on a different approach. 'I should probably introduce myself. My name is Jade and I've opened a shop in the town. Not books,' she added hastily. 'It's next door to Yesteryear Antiquities.'

'Is it now,' said the man, who she presumed must be Mr Darcy, though at that precise moment she couldn't think of anyone she'd less like to see emerging in a clinging, wet shirt from a lake. 'Terrible business, that.'

'Oh, you mean Freddy Stott? Is he – was he a friend of yours?'

'I wouldn't say friend,' said Mr Darcy. 'A fellow business owner, certainly. Our paths generally crossed on those terms. I'm not a golfing man. Don't have time.'

'I suppose you would have dealings with each other, as your businesses are complimentary,' said Jade. 'You could recommend each other, for instance.'

'One could,' said Mr Darcy. 'If one were so inclined. We didn't have as much common ground as you seem to think. My business is founded on provenance and quality, while Freddy's was—' He leaned forward confidentially. 'Best not to speak ill of the dead.'

'I quite agree,' said Jade. 'Well, it's been lovely talking to you, but I must get on. Good day.'

'What sort of shop do you—' Mr Darcy said as she pulled open the door, but the bell drowned the rest. *He can find me if he wants to. I haven't lied. Maybe I haven't told the whole truth, but I haven't lied. And he's clearly no fan of Freddy.* She resolved to make notes on the conversation as soon as she had a spare moment.

She returned the way she had come, then got changed, shook her hair out and descended to the shop. *Still time to make a drink and open for nine thirty.*

Her hope of making notes was frustrated, though. While there were fewer customers, they came in a persistent trickle, asking questions, initiating conversations about the properties of crystals, or sharing their thoughts on Aleister Crowley. Jade fielded them as best she could, where possible referring them to resources in the shop, and hoping she wasn't talking rubbish.

*I must top up that book order*, she thought, as a woman with a peroxide crop brought two copies of *The Joy Of Crystals* to the desk. 'One for me and one for my sister,' she announced. 'She's very into healing.'

'That's wonderful,' said Jade. 'Cash, card, or phone?'

As the broomstick ticked towards lunchtime, the number of customers in the shop increased. Jade leaned on the counter with the dregs of her tea and let her gaze roam around the room, settling first on one customer, then another. *I'm not paranoid*, she told herself. *I don't seriously think anyone here will shoplift, and I've seen no signs so far.* She remembered the woman who had fled from Fi's barge. *It doesn't hurt to keep an eye out.*

She scanned the shop. *Not staring, just taking in what's going on.*

As her gaze reached the door, it opened and Inspector Falconer, this time in a navy suit, entered. His eyes found her immediately and he walked over. 'Ms Fitch.'

'Inspector Falconer. How may I help you today? A dreamcatcher, perhaps? Pack of tarot cards?' A pair of young women who looked as if they should be in school giggled at the rear of the shop.

'Funnily enough, that's what I've come to ask you about,' said the inspector. 'We've had a few calls.'

'What sort of calls?' Every customer Jade could see was paying attention to them.

'Various people have expressed concern,' said the

inspector.

'About what, exactly?'

'The type of goods you're purveying, Ms Fitch. People have mentioned black magic. Voodoo. Curses.'

'What rubbish! Nothing in the shop could possibly do anyone any harm.' She felt like saying *As if anyone believes all that hokum*, then caught the eye of a customer and managed not to. 'You're very welcome to inspect any of my goods and draw your own conclusions. There's nothing you couldn't buy perfectly openly on the internet.'

The inspector raised an eyebrow. 'Nothing under the counter or in the back room?'

Jade stared, then beckoned to him. 'Come and check if you don't believe me. Nothing behind here: there isn't room. If you want to rummage in the back, be my guest.'

'I didn't mean it literally,' said the inspector.

'So what did you mean? Coming into a busy shop and hinting that my business isn't above board – has someone put you up to this?' Jade sensed the whole shop watching her, but she didn't care. 'I'd have thought you had better things to do, Inspector Falconer.'

'I happened to be passing,' said the inspector, his face pink. 'I'm sure you'll appreciate that at the present time, feelings are running high.'

'I expect they are.' Jade wished she were an inch or

two taller so that she could look down on him. 'This may surprise you, but what's happened is on all our minds, not just yours. I for one would welcome a speedy resolution to the matter, and I'd be very interested to know what you're doing to progress that.'

'Let's strike a bargain, Ms Fitch,' said Inspector Falconer, and his voice was cold. 'I won't presume to interfere in your business, provided you don't interfere with mine. This is a criminal investigation, not *Murder She Wrote*. Good afternoon.'

Jade eyed the clock, which showed ten minutes to twelve. 'Morning, I think you'll find.' But the inspector was already heading out of the shop.

Once the door had closed, a small ripple of applause came from the back of the shop. Jade grinned and mimed brushing dust from her hands, though she was vexed. *How dare you come in here and badmouth my business?*

The two young women came to the counter. 'That told him,' said the one on the left. 'Good for you.'

'Um, thanks.' They continued to stand there. 'Can I do anything for you?'

The one on the right leaned forward. '*Have* you got any other stuff? You know . . . under the counter?'

Jade's eyes narrowed. 'As it happens, and as I told the inspector, no.' Then she lowered her voice. 'What exactly would you have in mind?'

They looked blank. 'Dunno,' said the one on the

140

right. 'I just wondered, what with the inspector saying.'

Jade considered. Was it worth ordering in some mildly racy literature – shifter romances, that sort of thing – and offering it to customers who would appreciate it? Perhaps she should ask Fi's opinion. 'I'll bear your interest in mind,' she said, and reached for her notebook. 'Could you leave your name and number?'

# CHAPTER 16

'Will you be all right if I go out for my lunch?' said Fi.

'It is what it is,' said Nerys. 'If tourists want to nose about for something that's not there, I'll let them fill their boots. But if it's anyone from town, I'll tell them to wind their necks in.'

Visualising someone pulling a giraffe's head from a boot made Fi want to giggle, but Nerys's arms were folded so tightly that her hands might meet at the back, so she opted for reassurance. 'It's calming down. I'll only be gone an hour.'

Nerys uncrossed her arms and revealed a bracelet made of large crystal beads. 'That's pretty,' said Fi.

'Liam got it for me last Christmas,' said Nerys, twirling it. 'It's a bit heavy, but maybe it'll protect me against ghosts. I should go to that Jade's shop and ask. I bet that's the safest place in town right now.' Her worry appeared to lift. Fi wondered if Nerys was thinking of asking Jade for a job, leaving Fi with no one but Geraldine on Mondays. Then Nerys's frown returned. 'Unless Freddy's ghost is trying to get in from the shop next door, 'cos he was fighting with her when he collapsed.'

'They weren't fighting,' said Fi. 'Not exactly. And he never made it back to his shop.'

'Kev says ghosts don't always manifest where they died. They often appear in places where they suffered emotional trauma.'

'You do know that Kevin's been running ghost walks for twenty years and has never actually seen one, heard one, or even felt a shiver, except when he's not making enough tips.'

'I hear what you say, but—' Nerys shrugged. 'Moving on, any offers today?'

A minute or two later, Fi emerged onto the towpath, straightened the *BOOK BARGE OPEN* sign and checked that the large one in the window, which said *If you wish to sell me books, please enquire during opening hours. Please do not leave boxes outside*, was unobscured.

She had fifty-five minutes before Nerys would start panicking. Smoothing down her short summer dress, she made her way towards town.

Hazeby was a tourist's dream, with winding lanes and cobbled streets, a mixture of half-timbered buildings with upper jetties shadowing the pavements, sleek symmetrical Georgian merchants' houses, Victorian brick terraces and Gothic-style villas, a Victorian theatre with Art Nouveau twiddly bits, an Edwardian library with more twiddly bits, and a tiny 1930s Art Deco building, which had somehow survived nearly one hundred years as an independent cinema.

Fi walked along, taking it in as if she were seeing it for the first time. She had been full of hope for a new start with Dylan. She knew he would begin his high-school education with kids he didn't know, but he was unlikely to be the only one and had always socialised well. He could be part of realising a dream she'd had since she'd been a student: to open a quirky bookshop and live in it. A pretty little town was the perfect place to do that. A place where nothing happened and everyone was friendly.

How silly to assume that people were any different in a small town. Within a few months, Fi had discovered that illogical loyalties and petty grievances thrived in Hazeby, as they had in the Reading suburb where she'd lived before. There were the same love affairs and scandals, the same family feuds. The difference was that some of the ones in Hazeby went back centuries.

Before, it hadn't mattered. Fi and Dylan had joined clubs, made friends. She'd attended civic meetings as a businessperson and learned what to say or not to say – and to keep out of things that didn't concern her. Now, she wasn't so sure. Maybe she should have paid more attention to those illogical loyalties and petty grievances.

She passed a blackboard propped outside the Swan pub.

*GHOST WALKS!*
*TUESDAYS, THURSDAYS 2pm.*
*FRIDAYS, SATURDAYS 9pm*
*Discover Hazeby-on-Wyvern's dark and spooky past.*
*Ancient and modern*
*and very modern!*
*£8 for over-16s. £5 for 12-16. £4 for under 12s at parent's discretion.*

Beneath was a map of the route. Just as the words 'and very modern' had been recently added, so had a loop to Fi's part of the river.

She found hand sanitiser and a tissue in her bag and erased both words and loop.

'Here!' Kevin strode out of the Swan, pint of beer in hand. 'You can't do that.'

'I'm protecting a fellow entrepreneur,' said Fi, patting him on the arm hard enough for his beer to spill. 'The police would be *very* interested that you're profiting from Freddy's death so soon. They might

145

wonder if someone had set it up…'

Kevin paled. 'Hadn't thought of that. Er, thanks. Maybe in six months.'

'Maybe.'

She left him and continued down a pretty side street. It had been built sometime around the late nineteenth or early twentieth century, and the shop fronts had large panes in heavy frames with ornate names above. While many still capitalised on the age by looking as old-fashioned as possible – a toy shop, a sweet shop – a few by their nature combined old and new. One had Edwardian tiles around the door with stylised flowers in shades of arsenic green, and *F Reilly & Sons Dispensing Chemist* in Art Nouveau script over the window. The window display was of fancy toiletries, patent medicines and herbal remedies, and on the pane were the words *Independent Pharmacy* in a modern font. Feeling guilty, since she normally went to the very un-independent Boots closer to the boat, Fi opened the door. Clearly some ancestor of Roger Reilly had been a qualified pharmacist, but was Roger? For all Fi knew, they hired someone to do that job and the family money came from the counter stuff.

'Afternoon!' said the young woman behind the counter. 'Can I help you?'

'Afternoon,' said Fi. 'Just, er…' Her mind went blank. Neither she nor Dylan often needed a

146

prescription, and when they did, she'd never thought to check that the person dispensing it was qualified. More to the point, she was blank as to what she could pretend to look for. 'Bath sets. For a gift.' She spun round and realised she was standing next to a shelf full. That wouldn't help her with Roger's qualified status. She selected a gift set claiming to induce calm and inner peace. Maybe it would work on Annie. 'And, er... I wanted, um, an antihistamine. I hoped you could advise me.' She stepped up to the counter. 'I didn't get on with the last one I took.'

'Maybe it's best if you talk with the pharmacist.'

The pillars on either side of the counter displayed notices about vaccination programmes, blood tests, health advice... On the wall were framed certificates. Fi half leaned over the counter. Yes, one of them said Roger Reilly.

'Fi?' The man himself was before her. 'How can I – what are you doing?' Even though she'd stepped back, he turned to what she'd been staring at, then addressed the young woman. 'Sam, can you go to the office and see if the surgery's sent any prescriptions? The rush will start soon.'

'Oh yes, of course.' The young woman left.

'Are you checking up on me, Fi?' he said slowly, his eyes piercing hers.

'I was just, er, checking who was the pharmacist on duty today.'

147

'This isn't Boots,' snapped Roger. 'There's only me.' He leaned forward and lowered his voice. 'Don't think I don't know what people are saying about me and Amy and Fre—' He swallowed. 'About *possible* motive and definite means. Here was I, sorry that you'd been caught up in Freddy's death. Never for one moment did I think you'd suspect me of killing him. Or implicating you.'

'Roger, I—'

'Twenty-three pounds for that bath set, please, and if you want to discuss antihistamines, please bring in the one you reacted to. Card or cash? Loyalty card? No, clearly not. Loyalty evidently isn't your thing.'

A few minutes later, her face still burning, Fi entered a tiny pub in a narrow lane. In the daytime, it was usually full of tourists. Hopefully Fi could eat a quick lunch in peace without anyone but the bar staff noticing her. She ordered a brie and cranberry sandwich, took a cup of coffee to a tiny table and shoved the bag with the bath set underneath. She unlocked her phone to ask Stuart to join her, then realised she didn't want to talk to anyone. She didn't really want the sandwich. She sipped at the coffee and crossed her legs, kicking the bag as she did so. A scent of perfume drifted up and the image of Roger's stricken face returned. Her cheeks burned again.

'Abracadabra,' said the landlord, placing the sandwich in front of her. 'And that's magic!'

Fi stared at him, then at the plate. Cranberry oozed from the severed sandwich and the salad garnish was lurid green.

'Eat up, love,' he said. 'It won't poison you!' Then he chuckled. It *was* a natural chuckle, wasn't it? She managed a wobbly smile.

His head was on one side, his eyes appraising. Were other customers watching? Weren't some of them people she knew?

'I'm a bit behind,' she said, looking at her watch even though she couldn't read it all of a sudden. 'I'll have to wrap this up and go.'

The landlord shrugged. 'Enjoy it by the river while you can, eh?'

*While I can?* thought Fi. *What does he mean?* Forcing another fake smile, she wrapped the sandwich in her paper napkin and rushed out.

After a few yards she heard someone calling 'Hey!', but didn't turn. It wasn't for her. It couldn't be for her. She walked faster as she neared the boat and climbed gratefully into the bookshop. She put the sandwich in the fridge for Dylan to have later, and since there were no customers, told Nerys she could go early. Then she opened another paper bag and scribbled – no words, just twisting, blotting doodles. *What was I thinking? I shouldn't be investigating. I'll alienate everyone who's on my side if I carry on. I'll tell Jade we must stop and leave it to the police.*

Out of the corner of her eye, she saw something flutter into the boat from the wheelhouse. She glanced up: occasionally a bird got in and caused havoc by fluttering around in panic. There was no bird, though. Maybe a leaflet from the wheelhouse had blown down. She went to look.

On the floor was an envelope.

Fi collected it then climbed into the wheelhouse. Any of the various people outside could have dropped the envelope in. She leaned against the wheelhouse door and opened it.

*You and your friend should stop poking your noses in. Don't think you couldn't be next.*

Fi looked out. Nerys was making her way back to town, tapping on her phone. People lounged on the grass, while others jogged or cycled in the distance. Some she recognised, others she didn't – or couldn't, because of what they were wearing and the way they were facing. One of them must have thrown this in. One of them was threatening her and Jade.

Fi gritted her teeth. *Maybe I won't tell Jade I want to stop,* she said to herself. *I'll tell her that I'm carrying on regardless. No one's telling _me_ what to do. And I suspect they can't tell her, either.*

# CHAPTER 17

Jade sat at the counter with her phone, browsing the Amazon charts. Romance . . . paranormal romance… She was hesitating between vampires and werewolves when a thirty-something woman in jeans and a stripy top came to the counter, holding two spell books and eyeing Jade as if she were an uncaged lion.

'Excuse me? I'm very sorry to disturb you, but I wondered if I could have some advice.' She put the two books on the counter, side by side. 'Which of these would you recommend?'

Jade looked at the books, then at the customer, who seemed to wither slightly under her scrutiny. 'Well, I stock them both, and each is good in its own way. My advice is that it depends what you want to use them for and how much . . . *equipment* you have.' She tapped *Spells For Beginners*. 'If this is new to you, I would recommend this one. This one' – she motioned at *Shape Your Future With Spellcasting* – 'is likely to be more advanced.' She willed herself to keep a straight face. 'Perhaps you could try putting your hand on each book and seeing which one calls you.'

'Oh yes,' the woman breathed, doing as Jade suggested. She frowned. 'Yes... This one.' She pushed *Spells For Beginners* towards Jade. 'Thank you ever so much.'

'My pleasure. Cash, card, or phone? Would you like a bag?'

'Is it a plain bag? If so, yes please.'

Jade opened the counter drawer, found a plain brown bag and slipped the book inside. 'Do come back and let me know how you get on.'

'Oh yes, I will,' said the customer. She handed over a ten-pound note and hurried to the door, clutching the bagged book.

'Want your penny?' called Jade.

The customer shook her head fervently and made a swift exit.

*Maybe I need a back-door service*, thought Jade. She made a note on a fresh page of the notebook: *Private/discreet service for shy customers.*

She surveyed the shop. It was comparatively quiet, with two customers browsing. Stealthily, she reopened the drawer and brought out the second half of her ham sandwich, then unlocked her phone and plumped for vampires. She was about to take a bite when the door creaked open and Fi slipped in.

'Hello,' said Jade. *Why is she here?* Then she realised that Fi could help with the whole book question – including whether she'd mind if Jade started selling more books.

Then she saw Fi's expression: a strange mixture of defiance and fear, like someone willing themselves to touch a tarantula. 'What can I do for you?' she asked.

Fi surveyed the shop, pausing slightly at the two customers, who were still browsing. 'I hoped you might be available for a short consultation.'

Jade's eyebrows shot up. *I don't do tarot and palmistry stuff*, she mouthed.

*I know*, Fi mouthed back. She reached into her bag and put on a thin disposable glove, then produced a piece of paper. Keeping it close to her body to shield it from view, she unfolded it and showed it to Jade. As she did so, she held out the palm of her other, ungloved hand.

Jade's other customers were openly staring. She pretended to inspect Fi's hand. 'I see. Normally, I'd suggest you take a wart to the pharmacist, but…' She paused as if undecided, then lifted her head and addressed the other customers. 'I need to perform a quick charm, but it has to be done in private. I can either ask you to leave the shop and wait outside for five minutes, or you can remain while we go into the

153

back room.'

The customers, two well-groomed women of indeterminate age, nodded hard. 'We'll stay,' one said. 'I promise we'll behave.'

'Of course we will,' said the other. 'If someone comes in, we'll tell them that you're, um, performing a ritual.'

Jade smiled. 'I knew I could rely on you,' she said. 'Don't worry about guarding the shop: I have my own measures.' She waved a hand at the door that led to the back room. 'Come this way, please.'

Fi waited until the door was closed and they had both sat down at the table before speaking. 'What should we do?'

'Let's see that note again,' said Jade. 'Don't worry, I won't touch it.'

She peered at the note. Block capitals, shaky, written in black biro – could have been written with the opposite hand. Paper torn from a spiral-bound notepad, the kind you could buy in almost any shop. 'Not many clues,' she said. 'Was there an envelope?'

'Yes, but it was blank. Someone dropped it in through the wheelhouse twenty minutes ago. It's probably got my prints all over it. I was going to ignore it and carry on regardless, but that felt unfair as it concerns you too.' She looked up at Jade. 'Have you had one?'

'Nope,' said Jade. 'That's probably only because it

would be harder to pop a note through the door without being seen. The high street is busier than the walkway by your boat.'

'The towpath,' said Fi, automatically. 'Anyway, what shall we do?'

Jade shrugged. 'Go into hiding?'

'Don't be ridiculous,' said Fi, frowning. 'This isn't a laughing matter. We've been threatened.'

'Do you want to take it to the police?' Jade read the note again: ...*poking your noses in...* 'Actually, best not. We don't want the police thinking that we're doing their job. Even if we are. Ooh, that reminds me. Did you get any intel from the pharmacy owner? The one whose wife Freddy was—'

'He *is* the pharmacist,' said Fi. 'I saw his certificate. But I don't think it was him. He was so hurt that people thought he might have done it. He really seemed to be in pain. On top of the gossip about his wife, of course…'

'Mmm,' said Jade.

'You don't know him,' said Fi.

Jade lifted a hand in submission. 'I popped into the other bookshop this morning. While Mr Darcy' – she couldn't help a snigger – 'isn't a fan of Freddy, he wouldn't demean himself so far as to actually bump him off.'

'I suppose we're finding something out,' said Fi. 'Even if it's who didn't do it.'

'True,' said Jade. 'From now on, though, stick to stuff that people won't notice, since you've been given a warning and we can't tell the police. If there's any legwork needed, I'll do it.'

'You were in the letter too!' exclaimed Fi. '*You and your friend.*'

'They might not have meant me,' said Jade. 'You must have other friends. Besides, we hardly know each other.'

Fi looked startled. 'No, but we were together in the boat when – when it happened. That's probably what the person is thinking of. And if they're on to us, and they've already murdered Freddy…'

The pause hung in the air between them. 'Fine,' said Jade. 'I'll be careful. You be more careful. One murder in this town is quite enough.' She got up. 'I'd better get back to the shop. Thanks for coming and warning me. Although in future you should probably use the back door.' She sighed. 'It would be much easier if we could text each other like normal people.'

She marched to the door and opened it. The two customers had been joined by another very similar-looking one, to whom they were whispering. They started guiltily when she appeared.

She made a sweeping gesture to Fi. 'Say the phrase I taught you three times a day and it will keep shrinking. If it hasn't gone in three days, come back and see me.'

'I shall.' Fi inspected her palm. 'I think it's smaller already.'

'Excellent,' said Jade.

The customers observed Fi's progress to the door, then began whispering again. One approached the counter. 'Do you happen to have any resources on home remedies? It's so hard to get an appointment at the doctor's these days.'

'I do,' said Jade, walking to the section which she privately called *Snake Oil and Horse Pills* and picking up a book called *Herbology*. She handed it to the woman. 'But if you're worried about a symptom, go to the doctor or the pharmacist. There's only so much this can do.' She retreated to the counter and watched the three of them pore over the book, heads together.

'I've got a lovely rosemary bush,' murmured one. 'I don't think the supermarket stocks rue, though.'

'The health-food shop might,' whispered another.

Quietly Jade opened her notebook and wrote: *Investigate stock of health-food shop. Could collaborate. Any garden centres or plant nurseries?* She closed it as the women came to the counter, one carrying *Herbology* and a small cauldron. 'I'm sure the pestle and mortar would be fine, but...'

'No need to explain,' said Jade. 'It makes sense to have the right tools for the job.'

'Yes, it does!' The woman beamed at her.

'You don't have any more copies of that book, do you?' asked the new customer.

'Unfortunately, I don't,' said Jade. 'But I can order one in and ring you when it comes. Could I take your name and number?'

Once the customers had gone, twittering like starlings, Jade turned the shop sign to *Closed* and added a note saying *Replenishing energy: reopening 2.15.* She made a fresh cup of tea, finished her sandwich, which was slightly stale, and ate an apple for variety. Even so, she wasn't satisfied. Her mind refused to rest, and she felt twitchy.

*You need a walk*, she told herself. *That's all it is. Take your mind off the murder stuff and have a break from the shop. Buy yourself a bar of chocolate. You deserve a treat.*

*Yes*, she agreed with herself. *Serotonin.* She got her bag, locked the shop, and stepped into the street.

The sky had clouded over, which Jade took as a reflection of her own slightly troubled state. *That note probably isn't even from the murderer. It's probably some idiot trying to make trouble and scare Fi. People are like that sometimes, wanting to keep the story going. As if a murder isn't enough.*

She huffed, saw a newsagent's, and popped in for a Twix and a copy of the local paper. Remembering the woman who had paid for her spell book in cash, she did the same. *Best not to leave a trail*, she thought,

158

feeling very competent.

Back in the street, she pushed up a finger of the Twix and took a bite, mooching along and taking in the atmosphere. It seemed less busy than usual, possibly because of the less-than-perfect weather.

*Are you really bothered about that note?* she asked herself.

*No, but I think Fi is. She's caught between wanting to investigate and wanting to protect herself. Understandably. She's got a young boy.*

*You've got a young man.*

*That's different. Hugo can more than take care of himself. And so can I. So it's up to me to take the next step. We've eliminated book guy and pharmacist, so the only one left is pest-control man.*

She considered calling him in for a suspected mouse infestation, but that would cost money. While she was doing well at the moment, buying more stock was eating into her profits. *How else can I get to him?*

Over the road was a black noticeboard with *Parish Notices* in gold letters at the top. Jade crossed to examine it. As she got closer, the words *SOCIAL EVENING* jumped out at her in bright green letters, flanked by – were those crossed golf clubs?

*SOCIAL EVENING*
*HAZEBY-ON-WYVERN GOLF CLUB*
*THURSDAY 23RD JUNE, 7:30-11 pm*

## ALL WELCOME

Beneath was a photograph of a long, low building surrounded by well-tended greenery.

*Come and visit our delightful golf club, normally open to members only.*

*Sample the convivial atmosphere in the clubhouse, chat to our members, and learn the benefits of regular, gentle exercise. The club shop will be open and our golf pros will be available for consultation.*

*If the weather is fine we will offer a moonlight tour of our immaculate 18-hole golf course.*

*Ladies: no stilettos on the course, please.*

Jade grinned and popped the rest of the Twix finger in her mouth. *A golf-club social, eh? The perfect opportunity.* She took out her phone, pretended to message someone, and snapped a picture of the notice. *Fi has to keep a low profile, so she can't go*, she thought, putting her phone in her bag and moving on. *But there's nothing to stop me. And it's only a few days away.* She carried on down the street, mentally going through her wardrobe.

# CHAPTER 18

Back at the boat, several customers were mooching around. Fi had taken up Stuart's offer of help by asking him to mind the boat for half an hour while she popped out. Now he was schmoozing someone into buying a selection of management manuals, including one called *Breaking The Bucket Wall* which had been the go-to book for Wyvernshire Council's management training course until someone realised it was a parody.

'Have there been any notes, messages, phone calls?' she asked, after he'd sold the lot.

'Nope. Not unless you count the barmaid from the Vine dropping off a bag of fancy toiletries that you left under a table in the pub. A present? They don't seem quite your thing.'

'For my mother-in-law.' Fi relaxed. That was why someone had been calling her. It hadn't been sinister at all. 'You look like you're enjoying yourself.'

'I always enjoy it when you ask me to stand in,' said Stuart. 'I might rent some office space here instead of working at home.'

'You'll be welcome if you can shift those sorts of books. Although I feel a bit guilty about the bucket one.'

'I told her to read it last. By then, she'll get the joke.'

'You popped something else in her bag. What was it?'

'A gift for the shop from yours truly: a notebook with the book-barge logo and your website address, for ordering books, book news, and Fi's Fascinating Blog. I wanted a synonym for "blog" that began with F, but—'

'Wait! Stop! There's barely anything on my website. I don't have a blog. What if she looks it up?'

'Better start writing one, then.' Stuart grinned. 'It's an impetus to action. You've got in a rut, and now you've got Freddy's death hanging over you. You can't write about that, obviously, but you can write *something*. In the meantime, you look done in. I don't have any face-to-face appointments until after four and Dylan will be home well before then. Go for a run or a cycle or a drive. Take a break.'

Fi shook her head. 'I can't find something the police are asking for. At this rate they'll close me down, confiscate my devices and lock me up till I crack. I've told them I'm stuck until Geraldine returns, but I'm not sure they believe me. If I were a less rational person, I'd think it had magicked itself into invisibility. Maybe I can find it if I look hard enough.'

'Haven't you looked already?'

'A million times.'

'Then go away. Shake your brain cells back in place and it'll come clear. Shoo. I'm enjoying playing shopkeeper.'

'Don't you have sums to do?'

'I can do my sums between selling. See you at quarter to four.'

Fi drove out of town. Lanes twisted through fields, villages and farms in the sunny countryside. Larks and swallows swooped in a clear blue sky. Her thoughts remained glued together, though, tumbling in an incomprehensible cycle. The book, Freddy, the threatening note...

She tuned the radio to a nineties music channel and increased the volume to drown the turmoil. After a while, she drove into a bigger town further up the Wyvern, parked and checked her phone. Just a reply from Dylan, saying that he'd come straight home if they didn't put him in detention for answering her message.

Stuck worrying, her brain still wasn't releasing any

memory of where *More Magic* had come from. It was no good: she'd have to go through her laptop for the thousandth time. However, since she was here, she might as well go to the big Oxfam bookshop and see if they had anything of interest.

She entered the charity bookshop and breathed a deep, calming breath. Centuries of other people's thoughts, ideas, dreams and experiences nestled in a cave of pre-loved possibilities. Almost immediately she found an early edition of *Cider With Rosie* at a fair price and 1930s hard copies of the first five books in the Chalet School series, which would delight one of her regulars. She felt at peace.

'Hello, Ms Booker,' said Inspector Falconer.

All the calm dropped away.

'Oh. Hello. I didn't expect to see you here.' A cold thought struck her. He must be going round all the bookshops to check if they'd sold her *More Magic*. What if someone said they had and she'd completely forgotten? She'd look like a liar rather than simply incompetent.

'Nor I you,' said the inspector. 'I thought you'd be selling, not buying.'

'Someone's covering for me at the boat. I'm having an afternoon off. Things are...'

'Overwhelming?' His unexpected sympathy made her take him in more carefully. He wasn't in a suit, but blue chinos and a short-sleeved shirt. His tanned arms

164

looked strong. He was carrying a pile of books about dinosaurs and Mary Anning.

'What have fossils got to do with Freddy?' said Fi.

'Nothing. We're allowed time off too, you know.'

'So those books are for you?'

'The reading-age requirement for police officers is a little above this.' He grinned. 'No, it's for my son to give to his little half-brother for his birthday. Typical teenager, left it to the last minute. He's asked me to get a present before I pick him up from football.'

Fi grimaced and at the same time cursed herself. Presumably, his son's mother was with someone else now. But that didn't mean he wasn't, too. There was no wedding ring on the inspector's hand, but that meant nothing.

'I should let him deal with it himself,' said Inspector Falconer, 'but my ex-wife would say it was yet another example of me being too busy with work to have time for family life, even though it's not my family any more. Anyway, which do you recommend for a ten year old?'

Fi twisted her head to read the titles then pointed at one. 'That's the best of the bunch. Not too childish, not too dreary. And you don't have to explain to me about teenagers.'

'I know.'

She blushed. 'I suppose you know all about me.'

'You told me about your teenage son yourself,' he

said. 'But yes. We have to gather information on anyone involved in a suspicious death, however inadvertently.'

'Go on, then.'

He raised his eyebrows. 'You've been running that bookshop around four years. Prior to that, impeccable career for an established, respected profit-making organisation. No bankruptcies or judgements. No convictions. Not even a speeding ticket. Widowed twelve years. Member of a few of the civic groups in town, contributor at the town council meetings in support of tasteful, gradual change within the town. That's it. An upstanding citizen. Pretty much anyone could find that out.'

'Good grief, I sound so boring.'

He smiled a warm smile. 'A woman who has the initiative and imagination to escape a career in one of those plate-glass hamster cages and create something as lovely as your book barge could never be boring.'

She sensed him waiting patiently for her to speak. He seemed friendly and open. She ought to tell him about the anonymous letter, even though she and Jade had decided against it.

Then he said, 'However, imagination can backfire. Investigations should be left to professionals. There's nothing worse than clumsy amateurs muddying the waters: finding clues that aren't clues, seeing things that aren't there, wasting our time. It just leaves a bigger mess for us to clear up.'

'How thoughtless of them,' said Fi. He'd dismiss the note. 'Anyway, I must buy these, then take over from my son. I can't have you arresting me for overworking minors.'

He gave the merest hint of an eye-roll and Fi turned away. She didn't want to stand with him in the queue for any length of time, but when she looked again, he'd wandered into the mystical section of the shop. A cold sensation overrode Fi's irritation. Was he really off duty, or was he working semi-undercover, buying books so that he could ask the assistant oblique questions about a certain book and who might have bought it? She wasn't sure whether to go after him, or dump her books and run. Both would appear supremely odd.

Fi willed the customer in front of her to hurry, but he was donating a box of books and giving his details so that the shop could benefit further through Gift Aid. Despite her impatience, Fi couldn't help peeking at his books, then noticing the box itself. It was almost new, sturdy, only marred where the donor had removed a label which presumably included their address.

Something shifted in her head. Could *More Magic* have been in a box that someone, not realising or not caring that the book barge wasn't a charity shop, had dumped outside?

Fi made her transaction in a daze, then hurried home as fast as she could without drawing attention to herself.

She barely greeted Stuart and Dylan as she entered the shop and collected her laptop. What else had come in on the day that *More Magic* had been recorded? She ran her fingers down the list of titles and went to find them, visualising them in the box. Geraldine had brought it in while complaining about people's stupidity, then piled them up with the largest on the bottom and put the box aside, ready for recycling.

But it hadn't gone to recycling, had it? It had been a box worth keeping. Too big to send books to customers who'd bought online, but big enough for… Fi opened and shut the cupboards in the bedrooms and galley. No, it was too big for those. Then she went back into the bookshop.

Stuart, packing up, looked at her quizzically. 'Found the thing?'

'Not sure,' said Fi. 'Thank you, though. Going out was what I needed.'

'I'm always right.' He winked, kissed her cheek and waved goodbye as he left.

'You OK, Mum?' said Dylan. 'You look weird. What have I done?' His eyes narrowed. 'Or what will you make me do?'

'Get changed and have a snack,' she said. 'Then go

and game.'

'Are you ill?' said Dylan. 'Should I phone an ambulance?'

'I'm fine. Go on.'

She waited till he was in the home section, then unlocked the store cupboard in the corner of the shop. Inside were several boxes full of stock. One was less battered than the others. All the boxes had labels on, except that one. In several places the top layer was missing and the cardboard was a slightly different colour: yellowish, pinkish, bluish, as if dye from the labels had stained it.

Fi removed the contents of the box and inspected it. Was it the one *More Magic* had come in, or was she imagining things? Should she tell the police, just in case? Presumably they'd found it when they searched the boat, and discovered no trace of poison on it, so it should be of no interest. But what if she was wrong?

She picked up her phone, her fingers hovering. She could call the inspector, smug and bossy as he was. She could visit Jade and ask her opinion. Or she could bide her time till she was certain. Only... If the person who'd delivered the note thought she still had the box, was that a problem? Surely they'd assume she'd recycled it. If not, what would they do?

After a moment's hesitation, Fi cut the tape and folded the box flat. Then she slid it under the sofa bed

169

in the aft part of the boat, dislodging a hundred dust bunnies.

Seeing things that weren't there, muddying the waters, wasting police time?

She wasn't letting Inspector Falconer accuse her of that. She'd bide her time. Let him wait.

# CHAPTER 19

Jade cursed her lack of foresight as the taxi meandered along the country road that led to the golf club. She had been unable to book one before eight thirty, as everyone else had got in first, and it had turned up fifteen minutes late. 'Could you step on it?' she asked.

'What for?' asked the taxi driver, who in his diamond-patterned jumper looked as if he was planning to attend too. 'The golf club ain't gonna disappear. Although the free drinks might.'

'Free drinks?'

'They always lay on a free drink or two. Get people tipsy so they'll sign up.' He wheezed out a laugh. 'I know their tricks.'

Jade's nerves receded a little. She had planned on having a drink or two anyway, which was why she hadn't taken her car, and had lined her stomach with a couple of rounds of toast in preparation. That was all she had been able to manage. She looked down at herself. She hadn't wanted to overdress, but in her black skirt, sensible shoes and black sparkly top, not so different from what she would wear in the shop, she felt dowdy. *You're there to investigate*, she told herself, *not have fun.*

*A bit of fun wouldn't hurt*, her inner self whined. *I've barely had a break since I came to this place.*

'Here we are,' said the taxi driver, swinging the car left and heading down a long drive. 'Don't do anything I wouldn't do.' She saw him wink in the rear-view mirror and dug her nails into her palms.

The golf club looked just like the poster, with the addition of several posh cars outside. Jade paid the driver and got out. *Hopefully, if they're not drinking, there'll be some free booze left.* She smoothed her hair, checked she wasn't showing too much cleavage, and walked into the foyer. That was deserted, but a loud buzz of chatter came from behind two double doors. Jade took a deep breath and walked in.

She half-expected the noise to stop and everyone to stare, but nobody paid her any attention. That, perhaps, was worse. However, near the door was a table of champagne flutes filled with what Jade assumed was Bucks Fizz. Jade took one and, her first mission accomplished, studied the room.

It was filled with a mixture of large square tables

and smaller round ones, and packed with people. From the way they were sitting, relaxed and smiling, they all knew each other. And everyone was dressed up. The men were in tuxedos, some new and possibly hired, while others looked as if they had served their owners for thirty years or more. The women were sequinned and brightly coloured, like exotic birds.

'Great,' muttered Jade, 'just great.' She knocked back her drink, which tasted mostly of orange juice, and took another. *I'd probably have to sink a whole table full of these to feel anything*. She promised herself a proper drink later.

In the corner, a group of dinner-jacketed men were having an earnest conversation. Among them was the stooped form and fluffy white hair of Mr Darcy. *I'll say hello*, she thought, and wandered over.

If Mr Darcy had spotted her, he paid no attention. *Maybe he doesn't remember me. After all, I did dress down to visit his shop.* She hovered nearby, listening.

'They're a menace, an absolute menace. They come here and mess things up for the rest of us.'

'Blighters, they are. What are we going to do about them?'

*Oh dear*, thought Jade. *I'm not sure I want to get involved in this.*

'Frank's the man to ask.' They laughed. 'Come on, Frank, you're the expert. How do we get the moles off the golf course?'

Jade breathed a sigh of relief. Mr Darcy waved an irritable hand in front of his ear, then turned and saw her.

'Hello,' said Jade. 'I visited your shop the other day. Jade Fitch.' She held out her hand and after the slightest pause, he shook it.

'Yes,' he said. 'I remember you.'

'You said you weren't a golfer,' said Jade, before realising that wasn't the best thing to say at a golf-club social.

Luckily, he smiled. 'I'm not. It's a good opportunity to meet friends and network.'

'That's what I thought,' said Jade, 'seeing as I'm new in town.' She raised her voice. 'Would you mind introducing me to a few people?'

His brows knitted slightly. 'Of course. Geoffrey, Rupert, Frank, this is... Miss? Mrs?'

'Ms,' Jade said firmly. 'Ms Jade Fitch. I've just opened a shop in the town. Delighted to meet you. What do you all do? I know Mr Darcy runs the Olde Wyvern Booke Shoppe, but I've only met a few people so far.'

'Shall I begin?' said a lean, fiftyish man with steel-grey hair and a commanding manner. 'I'm Frank Menzies, I run a pest-control business, and this is my inaugural event as acting club captain. Are you interested in golf? A tour of the course begins in a few minutes.' He glanced at her shoes.

'Not sure a tour of the greens will entice anyone to join, Frank,' said a gloomy-faced older man. 'Not with the holes those damn moles have dug. Looks more like a snooker table.'

'Or a minefield,' said a man in a blue blazer. 'Anyway, what can we do about those moles? Don't tell me they're a protected species.' The men huddled closer, excluding her.

*So much for networking.* Jade stayed on the edge of the group, observing Frank Menzies. He seemed the sort of man who would be jovial most of the time, yet possibly ruthless when crossed. Was he the sort of man to arrange the elaborate poisoning of a rival? If anything, he seemed more likely to invite Freddy to come outside and settle the matter with his fists. With a sigh she drifted away, absentmindedly taking a swig of her drink.

She prowled among the tables but everyone was too engrossed in their conversation to welcome an intruder. *Maybe I should have asked the taxi to wait*, she thought, upending her glass again. As she did, she noticed a woman sitting alone at a small table in the corner. She was dressed to impress, in a cerise off-the-shoulder number accessorised with a sparkling choker and drop earrings, but she was moodily twirling the stem of her glass and staring at the table.

*At last*, thought Jade. *Someone who might welcome my company*. She strolled over. 'Excuse me, is this seat taken?'

The woman looked up. 'You can have whichever one you like,' she said. 'I don't mind if you take them all.'

'I meant to sit on,' said Jade. 'I'm new and I don't really know anyone.'

'Well, as you see, people tend to stick together,' the woman snapped. Then she attempted a smile. 'Sorry. I should be saying welcome to the town. I'm Amy Reilly.'

Jade tried to keep her face neutral, but inside she was screaming *Yes! Hit the jackpot!* 'Pleased to meet you, Amy.' She held out a hand. 'I'm Jade Fitch. I own a crystals and magic shop in the village: Crystal Dreams.'

'Don't pretend you haven't heard about me,' said Amy. 'Your face tells me you have.'

*Don't ever play poker.* Jade sighed. 'I'm sorry,' she said. 'I've heard a couple of rumours when people in the shop were talking. It's nice to put a face to a name. You seem a lively, friendly sort of woman. Not like this lot.' She dismissed the rest of the room with a wave of her hand.

'That's right,' said Amy. 'They aren't. They pretend they are, then the minute something happens —' She whipped a finger across her throat.

'Oh,' said Jade. 'Is it that bad?'

Amy giggled. 'I didn't mean they actually kill you,

176

silly. Just that they cut you dead.' Then her face crumpled. 'But someone did kill Freddy, didn't they? Maybe I should be worried.'

'Had you known Freddy for a long time?'

'Ever since I came five years ago,' said Amy. 'I already knew Roger, of course – I came here to move in with him – but I used to pop into Freddy's shop quite often to pick up one of his lovely antiques. To put a stamp on my new home. It was so plain.'

'And Freddy was kind to you.'

'He was,' said Amy. 'Right from the start he gave me a discount, and after a few months he invited me to private viewings when he had new stock in that he thought I'd like. There wasn't any harm in it, and Roger was so busy with the shop, what with the new Boots opening. I felt so alone.'

Gradually Jade became aware of a tinkling sound. Frank Menzies was tapping a champagne glass with a spoon. 'Everyone! The first tour of the greens will begin imminently, but while we are gathered together, I wish to propose a toast.' He held up his glass. 'To Freddy.'

'To Freddy,' the room echoed.

'To Freddy,' said Amy, a fraction late. Some people glanced round, then turned quickly back. 'See?' she exclaimed, draining what was left in her glass. 'They don't care one bit. Look, they're all talking again, except for Wendy. That's his wife.'

'Which one's Wendy?'

'There, in the black dress, with short grey hair.' Amy pointed to a table in the middle of the room. Wendy sat, hands in her lap, with a faint, resigned smile on her face while people talked to her. 'I never meant her any harm, but she's so quiet. So passive. Freddy said it was like being married to a wax doll. He wanted passion.'

'I want another drink,' said Jade. 'A proper one. What's yours?'

'Vodka martini, please,' said Amy. 'I'd rather have a porn star martini, but they don't do those. You'll have to go to the bar; there's no table service, for all their fancy ways.'

'Back in a minute,' said Jade. She set off at a sedate pace, taking a route that passed Wendy's table. 'What now, Wendy?' someone asked. 'Will you keep the shop on?'

Wendy shook her head. 'No, I'm giving it up. It was Freddy's pride and joy, and I wouldn't be able to do it justice. To be perfectly honest, I'm thinking of moving abroad. As one gets older one tends to seize up, and a warmer climate would be beneficial. A little place in the Dordogne, perhaps, with a gîte to rent out.'

Jade longed to linger and hear more, but forced herself onward to the bar. 'Vodka martini and a vodka and Coke, please. Diet Coke.' *Mustn't forget the diet.*

'Coming up,' said the barman. 'Martini for Amy Reilly?' He grinned.

'It is, actually,' said Jade. 'She was sitting in the corner all alone. I'm trying to cheer her up.'

'Well, if she hadn't been banging Freddy then she'd be here with her husband, wouldn't she?'

Jade stared at him. 'That's a bit harsh.'

'True, though. Roger used to be a regular and we haven't seen him for months. Not since word got around.' He reached for a cocktail shaker and shovelled ice into it. 'Just telling it how it is.'

The noise of the shaker drowned any opportunity for further conversation. Jade turned and scanned the room. *This lot would drink and gossip till the end of time. Bunch of dinosaurs.*

'Do you want these drinks or not?' asked the barman.

'Sorry,' said Jade. 'What do I owe you?'

'On the house,' said the barman. 'If you can keep Amy Reilly from causing a scene, it's the least I can do.'

'Gosh, thank you.' Jade took the drinks and weaved through the tables. Sadly, people were now talking at Wendy, not to her, but she didn't seem to mind, sitting with a serene expression on her face.

Amy was gazing into the middle distance, chin on hand. 'Here you go,' said Jade, sliding the martini towards her. 'My treat.'

'That's so kind of you,' said Amy. She looked as if she might cry, then grabbed the martini glass and took a gulp. Her eyes opened very wide and she coughed a dry little cough.

'Steady on,' said Jade, with a giggle. But Amy sat rigid and the dry little cough became first one retch, then another.

Heads turned. 'What's going on?' someone said.

'Let me through, will you?' said an exasperated male voice.

Jade raised her arm to give Amy a slap on the back, but it was caught in midair and a pair of strong hands forced her to her feet. 'First aid!' the man shouted. Jade twisted round and saw Inspector Falconer, wearing a tuxedo. 'Someone ring for an ambulance.'

'Let go of me,' Jade muttered. 'I haven't done anything.'

'Get away from the table,' said the inspector, as a woman in emerald-green satin rushed up with a first-aid kit. 'I'll let go of you on one condition: that you walk straight to the foyer without a fuss. I'll be right behind you, and if I have to I'll arrest you in front of the whole room.'

Jade swallowed, then walked to the exit, head held high so that she didn't have to see everyone's eyes on her. The double doors swung back and forth before closing. The noise from the room lessened considerably.

She faced the inspector. 'What am I supposed to have done?' she asked. 'You're not going to arrest me for poisoning Amy Reilly, are you?'

The inspector took a step closer. 'No. I'm arresting you for obstructing a police officer in the course of their duty. I've been watching you ever since you arrived. I hoped you were here to have a good time, but as soon as I saw you heading for Amy Reilly, I had my suspicions. I moved tables and heard you questioning her.' He took another step forward and bent his head to hers. 'And if you *have* attempted to poison her,' he murmured in her ear, 'things are about to get much, much worse.'

# CHAPTER 20

For the first time in ages, Fi fell asleep almost as soon as her head hit the pillow. She went to bed at ten, watched the constellation of Sagittarius circle the cabin ceiling just long enough to wonder what someone had been drinking the night they decided it was a centaur archer, then went out like a light. She dreamed of nothing . . . until her sleep was invaded by the sound of a distant train rattling over tracks, coming closer and—

Her eyes jerked open. Sagittarius was still slowly patrolling the cabin ceiling and her phone, ringing on silent, vibrated against her water glass. Her waking brain demanded *Who'd call at this time of night? What time of night is it, anyway?* She ticked people off a checklist of possible callers. *Gavin: dead. Dylan: in his cabin. Mum: never rings after nine.*

The phone stopped, then vibrated again. Fi swore,

and grabbed it before it exploded.

All she recognised about the number was that it was local. Her heart started to thud. 'Hello?'

'Is that Ms Booker?'

'Speaking.'

'This is Sergeant Roper from Hazeby police station. Inspector Falconer gave me your number.'

'Who? What?' Fi got clumsily out of bed, wrenched the cabin door open and knocked on Dylan's door.

A muffled voice called, 'Aw, Mum! You said I could play another hour on my game!'

Fi shook herself and put the phone to her ear. 'I'm sorry, Sergeant Roper, can you explain? This is' – she looked at the clock, which declared it was 11:30 – 'unexpected.'

'A friend of yours was arrested but is about to be released without charge. She wonders if you could collect her.'

'Arrested? A friend?' Fi ran through the possibilities and concluded that her friends were as boringly law-abiding as she was. 'I mean, of course. Which one?'

'Jade Fitch.'

Fi felt as if she'd downed a large black coffee. She barely knew Jade. What might she be doing, and getting Fi mixed up in, on top of everything else?

'*Are* you able to come? No one can take her and all

the taxis are up at the golf club. She can't walk at this time of night.'

'Yes. I'll be there in fifteen minutes. Tell her she won't be locked up for long.'

'They can't lock her up,' said Sergeant Roper, with officious indifference. 'She hasn't been charged, and if she had, she'd be bailed for that offence anyway. She'll be in the waiting area by the front desk. Do you want to speak to her?'

'Yes, please.'

After a pause, Jade said hello.

There was no point in being circumspect. 'What are you supposed to have done?'

'Obstructed a police officer.' Jade sounded weary and strained. 'So far, that's all.'

'Obstructed who? How?'

'Guess. I went to the golf-club do.'

Fi was about to ask *Why? Are you really that bored?* when she realised. Half the great and the good of Hazeby-on-Wyvern would be there. Jade must have gone to snoop without asking Fi to join her.

Irritation, concern, anxiety and exasperation filled Fi. She knew people, she could have helped with introductions, it would have been more natural. Did Jade not trust her, or did she see Fi as a weak link because of her reaction to that bruising conversation with Roger? But Jade could at least have told her what she was planning. If whoever poisoned the book *had* been at the social, what would they do to someone bumbling around and asking awkward questions? It must be hard to poison a book, but it would be relatively easy to poison a drink in a place full of people drinking more than they should. Stupid woman. What had she been thinking?

'OK,' said Fi, slowly. 'I'm guessing you socialised and tried to make new friends, and perhaps that was misinterpreted?'

'I'm glad *someone* understands.' She heard the relief in Jade's voice.

'You said "So far, that's all". What else did you do?'

'Nothing! I'll explain later.'

'I'll be there as soon as I can.'

The stark lights in the police station's waiting area were coldly disquieting, as if they were designed to put people on edge rather than comfort them. Jade, normally so feisty, seemed diminished: a forlorn figure in black, hunched in a hard plastic chair, half-heartedly watching someone very inebriated explain to the desk sergeant that he'd seen an alien buying dog food from the mini-mart. On the other side of the room, a middle-aged couple sat holding hands, the woman silently crying, the man grim-faced. Everyone looked grey under the strip lighting, and apart from the drunk, thoroughly miserable.

'Jade?' Fi's irritation ebbed a little. 'Why didn't

you tell me what you were doing? I could have helped. I thought we were—' She was about to say *in this together,* then realised what that would suggest to anyone lip-reading the inevitable CCTV footage. 'I thought we were friends. I could have come. Those networking dos are deadly.'

'I thought maybe you'd be there,' said Jade, standing up and shaking her head ever so slightly to negate her words, 'and if you weren't, it was because you didn't fancy it. I just wanted to network. I can do that on my own. I don't need a chaperone.' She leaned closer, presumably to mutter, but paused with her mouth half-open, looking over Fi's shoulder.

'I dispute that,' said Inspector Falconer. He was wearing a crisp white shirt but no tie, and particularly smart black trousers. 'A chaperone is *exactly* what you need.'

'Do you make a speciality of sneaking up on people, Inspector?' said Fi, her irritation returning. 'That's the second time today you've nearly given me a heart attack.'

'I wouldn't get tetchy if I were you, Ms Booker. And it's gone midnight, so technically I've only done it once today. So far. Now, I can't compel either of you, but would you both join me in a side room?'

'Yes sir.' Jade saluted.

'Don't be cheeky, Ms Fitch. If you'd like me to charge you, it's no skin off my nose. Perhaps I'll consider remand instead of bail. We're not allowed to keep people in the cells here overnight any more and the custody suite is forty miles away. Fancy that?'

'Come on,' said Fi, nudging Jade. 'Let's get this over with.'

In a side room as stark and daunting as the waiting room, Fi sat next to Jade, with Inspector Falconer on the other side of the table. Suddenly she was transported back to being Dylan's age, up before the headteacher for arguing over the length of her uniform skirt.

'Is something amusing you, Ms Booker?' asked the inspector.

'I'm just tired.'

'You can't be as tired as I am with you two.' The inspector tapped the table with his fingernails. 'I'm not a fool, Ms Booker. I've already warned Ms Fitch about playing detective. I thought you had more sense, but I can tell you're in cahoots. I don't understand why two intelligent women can't leave things to the police.'

'Who says we aren't?' said Fi.

'Did you know Ms Fitch was going to the golf-club social tonight?'

'No.'

'I already told you she didn't,' said Jade. 'I did it off my own bat.'

'But you've *both* been questioning people round

town. When a certain Mr Reilly came to visit his wife in hospital earlier, for example, he complained that "even Fi Booker" had been checking his credentials, and he hoped everyone would be satisfied of his innocence now.'

Fi's face burned again. 'Hospital? Amy Reilly? What's wrong with her?' She glanced at Jade, whose face had turned paler.

'She collapsed while we were talking,' said Jade, in a near-whisper. 'She took a sip of her martini and... I swear it didn't look as if she'd drunk strychnine. It was nothing like when Freddy died. Then I got dragged off and I don't know what happened next.'

'I didn't drag you off,' said Inspector Falconer, 'and what makes you mention strychnine?'

'Never mind that,' said Fi. 'How is she?'

'She's fine. She should learn to sip with more ladylike decorum and you should learn to address the police ditto.'

'I'm sorry,' said Fi. 'But Jade was there when she collapsed and might think the worst. You don't understand how traumatising it was to see Freddy that day. You could have told her Amy was OK as soon as you knew, rather than letting her think Amy might have died.'

'I only just heard,' said the inspector. 'That's the main thing I brought you in here to say. What with the snark, things went off track.'

'It's taken three hours to discover that her drink went down the wrong way?' exclaimed Jade.

'We had to eliminate other possibilities. Amy was already beyond tipsy before you spoke to her, and all the panic made her virtually incomprehensible.' The inspector sat back and scratched the little fair bristles coming through on his chin. 'I'm sorry it took so long to let you know, Ms Fitch. I hadn't appreciated how worried you were: you tend to give the opposite impression. Anyway, on the understanding that you have been detecting when you shouldn't, what have you found out?'

Fi exchanged glances with Jade, wishing she knew her well enough to guess what she was thinking. She sighed. 'Our theory is that the book's pages were laced with strychnine. It can't be easy to get hold of these days, though I haven't tried looking. So we focused on chemists, pest controllers and . . . possibly someone with access to old books with chemical formulae that could help the poisoner. *Was* it strychnine?'

'Yes,' said Inspector Falconer. 'How did you guess?'

'My son knows a medic,' said Jade. 'I told him what happened. They worked it out.'

'Right. Motives?'

'The usual,' said Jade, shrugging. 'Wronged

husband of a mistress? Professional jealousy?'

'Or possibly someone trying to scupper my business,' said Fi.

'You mean old Mr Darcy?' Fi expected the inspector to snort in derision, but he didn't. 'Yes, we're considering that. But *someone* who saw Freddy collapse visited Mr Darcy and asked odd questions, which forewarned him. You know what they say about being forewarned.'

Jade grimaced. 'I—'

'Please listen to me, both of you. Some of the pages of that book were, as you suspect, laced with strychnine, and—'

A thought struck Fi. 'That could have happened a hundred years ago, and this is a tragic accident.'

'It could,' said the inspector, 'and that was our first line of enquiry. However, all the indications suggest that it was done extremely recently. It's almost certain that whoever poisoned that book knew exactly how potentially lethal it was. And this means that assuming you didn't do it, Ms Booker, you might be the target.'

'But I—'

'All I want is for you *both* to be safe while I finish this wretched investigation and bring the right person to justice, but you keep impeding me.' Inspector Falconer leaned forward. 'So this is not a caution or even an official warning. It's a friendly request. Off the record, for the last time, I'm telling you to stop asking questions and putting people's backs up. Because if you don't, the worst thing you're risking isn't an official warning from me. A murderer is out there, and there's no reason for them to stop at one murder.'

# CHAPTER 21

Jade followed Fi out of the police station, her head in a whirl. 'Come on,' said Fi, taking a set of keys from her pocket. 'Let's go home.' She paused, studying Jade. 'Are you OK?'

Jade blinked. 'Yes, I'm fine.'

Fi scrutinised her with a thoroughness that made her want to turn away. 'You don't look fine, you look cold. It's probably shock. I've got something in the boot.' She led the way to a blue Fiesta parked at the end of a row, underneath a light. Jade had half-expected a quirky car – a 2CV or an old Beetle, or one of those little Fiats that looked as if they'd overturn on a sharp corner.

Fi opened the boot and handed her a navy fleece. 'Here, put this on. I know it's midsummer, but still.'

Jade did as she was told and got into the passenger seat. The car was clean, empty of the used parking tickets and chocolate wrappers that Jade never remembered to clear from her own door buckets. Fi got in the car and started the engine. 'It shouldn't take long at this time of night.'

'Thanks,' said Jade. 'For coming and getting me, I mean. Especially since we hardly know each other. There wasn't really anyone else to ring.'

'It's OK,' said Fi. The car moved slowly towards the exit. 'But you should come back with me and spend the night on the boat. You shouldn't be alone, not after all that.'

'I don't want to put you out—'

'There's a sofa bed in the aft cabin and a curtain to pull across and be private. We use it as a spare room. It's fine. To be honest, I'd rather not leave Dylan alone for longer than necessary.'

'I'm sorry,' said Jade. She bit her lip as guilt washed over her. *You idiot. What a stupid thing to do. You might have known something like this would happen. The shop's doing great, you had the chance to make a success of it, and you've ruined that.* She closed her eyes to keep the tears in. Luckily, Fi was concentrating on the road and didn't notice – or she was tactfully keeping quiet. After a minute or two, Fi switched on the radio – standard pop, at low volume.

Jade watched the world go by, dark and silent. It seemed no time until Fi parked up a few metres from the towpath. 'It's a short walk from here.' She led the

193

way to the boat, which loomed in the dark. The river was louder, too. 'I don't know if Dylan's awake or not – I expect he will be – but if you could be quiet coming in.'

Jade followed her along the gangplank. She could see lights in the main part of the boat.

'Where have you been, Mum?' She recognised the deep tones of a voice that hadn't been broken for very long.

'I was picking someone up,' said Fi. 'You've met Jade, haven't you? She owns Crystal Dreams.'

'The witch lady?'

'*No*,' said Fi, 'the owner of Crystal Dreams. She's staying over.'

'Oh. OK.'

'I wasn't asking for permission,' said Fi, descending into the boat and motioning to Jade to come too. 'You should be in bed, Dylan. It's school tomorrow.'

'It's work tomorrow for you,' said Dylan. Jade scrutinised him: tall, gawky, with hair the same colour as his mother's but different features. Maybe he took after his father. 'Can I get a snack?' he asked. 'I'm hungry.'

Fi sighed. 'Yes, but make it a quick one and then get to bed. No cheese toasties or quesadillas.'

Dylan sighed. 'You spoil all my fun. Night, Mum.' He waved at Jade. 'Night, Jade.'

'Goodnight,' said Jade. He turned and went into the private quarters.

Jade tried not to think about cheese toasties, but the damage was done. Oozing cheese, the dark lines where the bread had caught slightly, the rounded edges… Her mouth watered and her stomach growled.

Fi looked at her. 'You sound hungry. Did you manage to eat anything at the golf club?'

'I wasn't there long enough,' said Jade. 'Anyway, I didn't see any food. Not even a cheese and pineapple hedgehog.'

'I'll let Dylan get to bed, then forage,' said Fi.

'Thanks,' said Jade. 'I don't want to be a nuisance.'

'You're not,' said Fi. 'You've had a hard night. I'm sure you'd do the same for me.'

That made Jade grin. What were the odds of Fi going off on a harebrained mission and having to be rescued? 'Hopefully I'll never have to. You're far more sensible than me.'

Fi's lip curled, then she managed a rueful smile. 'Probably.' A door closed. 'The coast's clear. Why don't you sit down.' She pointed at the sofa and disappeared into the back.

Jade sat and eased off her shoes, which despite being sensible pinched her left heel. She rubbed it absentmindedly and made a face. *What a night. What a mess.* She leaned forward, elbows on knees, chin on hands. Were she and Fi really holding up the investigation by getting in the way? It was hard not to get involved, though, when the police didn't seem to be doing anything. Her mind went in circles, imagining herself and Fi chasing the criminal, the criminal chasing them, and the inspector chasing all of them...

The door opened and Fi negotiated her way round it with a tray. On it was a bottle of red wine, two glasses, and an assortment of food: a bowl of crisps, olives, crackers, two kinds of cheese and cherry tomatoes. She put it on a side table by the sofa and sat next to Jade. 'I just grabbed what I could,' she said. 'I didn't want to take too long in case Dylan came to see what we're up to.'

'You make it sound as if we're having an affair,' said Jade.

A brief laugh shot from Fi. 'I wouldn't know. But yes, what with sneaking in and out of your shop and now this... Maybe we should get burner phones.'

Jade stared at her. 'How do you know about burner phones?'

Fi waved a hand at the crime and thriller section. 'Plus TV, of course.' She picked up the wine bottle and twisted off the top. 'I assume you drink wine.'

'Oh yes.'

Fi half-filled the glasses. She picked them up and handed one to Jade. 'Cheers.'

The clink of the glasses sounded hollow to Jade.

'What are we drinking to, exactly? The end of our investigation? The probable end of my business?' She closed her eyes. *Tomorrow, I'll check the paperwork on the shop lease. Maybe I can end it early.*

'You're looking very serious,' said Fi.

Jade raised her eyebrows. 'Do you blame me? I got marched out of the golf club in front of everyone. Amy Reilly may be fine, but my business is dead.'

'Of course it isn't,' said Fi. 'Once everyone knows that Amy's fine, they'll see it was a mistake. An overreaction by the inspector.'

'Hmm.'

'They will. If anything, they'll probably visit your shop for a look around. I had loads of people visiting the boat: people who normally never would.'

'I just—' Jade sipped her wine, wondering how to say what was in her head. 'It's all very well for the inspector to tell us to keep our noses out,' she said. 'But when we're actually getting somewhere, and as far as we know they're not, it's impossible to sit on your hands and do nothing.' She reached for a handful of crisps.

'I agree,' said Fi. 'So, did you find out anything this evening?' She rolled her eyes at Jade's surprised glance. 'Yes, the inspector said not to do anything, but sharing what we know isn't *doing* anything, is it? Not really.'

Jade tried a crisp. Ready-salted. *Good.* 'Well,' she

said, when she could speak, 'I don't think for one minute that Amy Reilly has anything to do with Freddy's murder. She was so upset. She seemed to actually love him. Or maybe the presents and the attention, but it comes to the same thing. And I met the pest-control guy, Frank Menzies. He seems too straight down the line. I could see him telling Freddy to his face that he's a snob and a creep, not poisoning him.'

Fi stared into her glass, then drank some wine. 'Two more doors slam shut,' she said. 'I don't think Roger Reilly did it, or Mr Darcy at the bookshop.'

'So we're out of suspects,' said Jade. 'It isn't looking good, is it.'

They sat musing, silent apart from an occasional crunch and rustle as they snacked. Jade replayed the evening in her head, trying not to grimace as she recalled the snubs she had received, the closed-in groups... 'Could someone want to get hold of Freddy's shop?' she said. 'Or buy his house? I overheard his wife Wendy say that she was thinking of selling up and moving abroad.'

Fi's eyebrows drew together slightly. 'Oh? Last time I saw her, just after Freddy had died, she said she would seek comfort in her garden.'

'People can change their minds,' said Jade. 'Especially after something like this.'

'True,' said Fi. 'I remember how I felt when I

heard that Gavin had died. Well, had gone missing, at that point. It was ridiculous, really – we'd been separated for a while and I was divorcing him – but even so, I was a mess. I'd start doing one thing and switch to another, forget appointments, turn up on the wrong day. My brain couldn't hold on to anything.'

Jade stared at her, horrified. 'I'm so sorry. I didn't know.' *How else can I put my foot in it today?*

'You wouldn't.' Fi smiled a sad smile which faded quickly, like the flame of a near-spent candle. 'I don't broadcast it, for obvious reasons.' Then she grinned. 'You're missing an opportunity, Jade. You should be recommending healing essential oils or a spell to attract a new man.'

'Don't be daft,' said Jade. 'As if I believe any of that rubbish.'

'So why have you got a crystal shop?'

'I knew someone who ran one in my last place and she was doing really well,' said Jade. 'Business decision. Anyway, back to the point. Could Freddy's shop or his house motivate someone to kill him?' She huffed. 'That sounds thin even to me.'

'It does a bit,' said Fi. 'But it's the best we've got at the moment.' She sighed. 'I can't help feeling that we're missing something.' Then she checked her watch. 'Good grief, it's half one. Have some more food and finish your wine, and then we'd better get to bed. We'll have to sleep on it for now.'

# CHAPTER 22

An unexpected thump woke Fi from a deep sleep. She felt disoriented, out of kilter. It was unheard of for Dylan to be awake much before eight unless he was sick. Had she missed the alarm? She checked the time. 6:59: it was about to go off. She cancelled it and lay tense, listening.

Water lapped against the boat. Someone was calling 'pull' at regular intervals. She could hear the creaking of synchronised oars rolling in their locks and rhythmic, barely audible splashes. The steady thump-thump of a jogger sounded on the towpath and a bicycle bell rang. Ducks quacked and squabbled and gulls shrieked. Normal summer noises.

*Thump*. A muffled curse.

Why was there someone in the bookshop? Fi got out of bed, pulled on her dressing gown and stepped into the galley. On the table was a three-quarters empty bottle of wine, two glasses, empty but for dried wine-tears down the inside, and a stack of bowls and plates, empty save for crumbs. She stared for a whole two seconds, then the previous night returned in a flood.

Jade. The police station. The early-morning conversation. Of course.

In the bookshop, Jade, wearing a long shirt of Fi's, was sitting on the sofa nursing her left foot. She paused in her low steady swearing to stare up at Fi. 'Why do you have so many things lurking in the dark for people to stub their toes on?'

'It's not *that* dark and the light switch is just there. Were you trying to kick your way through to the loo?'

'I was *trying* to be quiet,' said Jade. 'But I didn't know if there were special boaty instructions for flushing, so I thought I'd wait till you got up and find the Wi-fi router instead.'

'Ah. Sorry if I sound grumpy. I need coffee before I can be polite first thing in the morning.'

'Fair enough.' Jade followed her into the living quarters. 'I'll pop to the . . . what's the proper boat name again?'

'Heads. But bathroom's fine. Here's a guest towel, then you can change in my cabin. Tea or coffee for when you're out?'

'Tea. It's not herbal or decaf, is it?'

'Do you want it to be?'

'Good grief, no.'

By quarter to eight, Jade was nursing a second mug of tea and watching Dylan absorb cereal. The disturbed night had invigorated him, if anything. He took Jade's presence in his stride, asked her a few questions about ghost-hunting without noticing that her answers were vague in the extreme, then told her at length what to stock to keep the Dungeons and Dragons contingent happy.

'Thanks,' said Jade, when she could get a word in.

Fi looked at the calendar and grimaced. 'Dylan, you've got a French exam today! And you were awake half the night!'

'*C'est rien, maman. Je suis incroyable en français.*'

'*Incroyable* as in "amazing", or as in your teacher won't be able to believe what you come up with? Hadn't you better get to school early? Shall I drive you?'

'*Non, merci! Je préfère mon vélo! À bientôt!*' Snatching up a piece of toast, Dylan grabbed his school bag and left the boat.

'Stay safe!' called Fi.

'*Arrête le fuss, maman!*' he yelled back.

Fi shook her head and put the kettle on again. 'Was Hugo like that?'

'He used to test me on the periodic table.'

'Blimey. Did you know it?'

'Nope.' Jade was pushing her empty mug about.

Fi took it and popped in a teabag. 'Let's go on deck. Fresh air will help us think.'

'I can't face it.'

'Fresh air?'

'Townspeople and boaty people. They'll all be looking at me. *Knowing*.'

Fi raised her eyebrows. 'It was the golf-club social you went to. Any early birds who aren't hungover will be at the golf club, golfing. Anyone on the towpath wouldn't have been at that do. I doubt many of the live-aboards would go, either.'

'You're a live-aboard, and *you* go to dinner dances at the golf club.'

'I've *been* to dinner dances,' Fi corrected as she refilled their mugs. 'The golf club hires out the venue to other groups. I went with the drama society. They put on plays at the theatre between professional productions.'

'You do acting?'

'If I could act, I wouldn't have made such a pig's ear of visiting Roger's pharmacy. No, I was dating an actor.'

'Oh.' Jade pulled a face. 'Sorry, I'm prying.'

'Don't be silly,' said Fi. 'It's not a secret. And he isn't the only person I've dated since Gavin died, but... In the end, our dreams weren't the same. It didn't work out.' *They never are*, she thought. *It never does*. 'Anyway, I can't exactly remember what we said last night, but I'm pretty sure it included not letting this get to you' – she raised her hand to stop Jade interrupting – 'because if you do, you can't think clearly and nor can I.'

'Everyone there will think—'

'You don't know what they'll think: you were in the middle of the action. If you were looking in, you'd just see the newcomer—'

'The witch woman.'

'Don't listen to Dylan. Anyway, coming from him and his friends, that's praise. Going back to what I was saying, you'd just see the newcomer networking. There are cliquey people here, like everywhere. But whatever Amy told you, others are quite the opposite. In normal circumstances, you'd probably have met nice people eventually yesterday evening. Another time, I'll introduce you.'

'There won't be another time. I need to leave. I don't suppose you understand.'

Fi closed her eyes, recalling the early days of the book barge, when she had no real idea of how to stop her dream turning into a nightmare; the last man she'd dated, who she thought might be able to mend her heart and then didn't; the abrupt rethink required to guide the business through lockdown while also coping with Dylan, cooped up in a space which suddenly felt too small for one, let alone two.

'People will have seen you chatting with Amy,' she told Jade, 'then they'd have seen her drink going down the wrong way and someone coming to help, then you leaving with a man.'

'I bet they all know he's an inspector,' said Jade, gloomily. 'So they'll assume I was arrested.'

'Maybe some did,' Fi conceded. 'But he was dressed up and people had been drinking, so hopefully most assumed he was your boyfriend, looking after you. People know you were here when Freddy collapsed, and from what I've heard, they know in detail about the convulsions.' Fi shuddered. 'Amy was just choking, so *they* wouldn't connect the two, but they might think *you* did and it was too much for you. I bet people visit your shop to check up on you and then buy stuff. People are very odd, and sometimes that's in our favour.'

'You reckon?'

Fi braced herself. 'For the record, I absolutely understand about wanting to run away. Once this thing with Freddy is over, if you ply me with wine, I'll pour it all out and you'll wish you'd never asked. But Jade, there are pluses to staying put and standing up to your embarrassments, and one of them is being around long enough to make friends. Real friends.' She lifted her mug in a toast.

'Maybe.' Jade didn't look convinced but clinked mugs anyway.

'So, back to business,' said Fi. 'Last night, you said Freddy's murder could relate to his house or business. His house is a detached place in a quiet road. I only know because I've visited on Open Garden days to see Wendy's latest designs. She's an amazing gardener.'

'According to Amy Reilly, Freddy called his wife a passionless wax doll.'

'His charms never cease, do they?' said Fi. 'I don't blame her for retreating into something else. I know I would.' *I did*, she reminded herself.

'His business?' said Jade. 'It seemed like a mishmash of junk to me, and so old-fashioned. I suppose the olde-worlde stuff goes down well with tourists, but…'

'But you can do olde worlde in a modern way,' said Fi. 'I agree. A lot more money could be made by doing it differently and applying panache. People suggested it to Freddy often but he wanted things as they'd always been. "Always" being since the seventies.'

'Was he covering something up?' said Jade. 'Was he handling stolen goods? Did he do the dirty on someone, and they sent him a poisoned antique book to… No, that doesn't work, because the book came here.'

Fi ran her fingers through her hair and pulled it a little. The more possibilities they thought up, the less likely they seemed. She glanced at the clock. 'Oh, drat. I'm opening soon and I haven't set up.'

'I haven't folded up the sofa bed,' Jade confessed. 'I wasn't sure how.'

'I'd forgotten that. There's a knack, but it helps to have two. Come on: battling with that might dislodge a memory.'

It did. As they forced the folded mattress into place the sofa shifted backwards, revealing the flattened cardboard box Fi had hidden there a few hours earlier.

'I knew I meant to tell you something!' She pulled it out and blew the dust off.

'You're behind with recycling?' Jade looked blank.

'No. I'm not a hundred per cent sure, which is why I didn't mention it to the inspector last night, but I *think* the book arrived in this box with a load of other, innocent books. People dump stuff occasionally. It's a real pain.'

'Any markings? Addresses?'

Fi shook her head. 'No. That's the thing: there are none. That seems odd. I can understand removing your own name and address, and maybe the sender's if they're a private individual. When the sender's a business, why bother?'

'How do you know it's a business?'

'Here, and here.' Fi showed Jade the rectangular coloured stains. 'Someone's peeled professional labels off.' She sighed. 'Or perhaps it's just come from an individual who collects stickers.'

'Wait a moment,' said Jade. She took the cardboard from Fi and turned it into a box. 'This reminds me of something. Hang on while I have another swig of tea. OK, now it's time for you to do some acting after all.'

'What?'

'Stand up, go back a bit, hold that box under your arm as if it's full of stuff, then walk towards me and sneer.'

'Sneer?'

'OK, you needn't sneer, but do it anyway.'

Fi shrugged and did as she was told.

'Freddy!' exclaimed Jade, eyes wide.

Before she could stop herself, Fi glanced at the area where Freddy had collapsed. She saw nothing and turned back, feeling ridiculous.

'Not Freddy's ghost, you daft bat!' said Jade. 'Freddy's box.'

'*His* box?'

'The first time I met the wretched man, he was carrying a box very similar to that, covered in little coloured labels dotted about just like those stains.'

Fi stared at it. 'But…'

'We have to tell Inspector Falconer.'

'But—'

Jade stabbed at her phone. 'Can I speak with Inspector Falconer? Yes, it's important. It's to do with

208

the Stott case… S-T-O… Yes, that's the one. Oh, is he? It's urgent, I have information… No, I want to speak to him personally… Jade Fitch. F-I-T— Yes, me again. Or he can speak with Fi Booker… Yes, the one who collected me. Will you pass it on? Cheers. Bye.'

'What on earth will Inspector Falconer say?' Fi stared at the box, wondering how much less like evidence it could look.

'He'll say thanks,' said Jade. 'At least, he will if he knows what's good for him.'

# CHAPTER 23

'Where are you going?' asked Fi, as Jade picked up her handbag. Her tone said *Don't leave me with this*.

'I'm going to the flat to get changed,' said Jade. 'I can't wait to get out of these clothes. I'll pop a note on the door and come back. If that's what you want.'

Fi looked relieved. 'Yes. Although you should open up later.'

'Maybe,' said Jade. 'See you soon.' She left the boat and walked along the gangplank, wincing as her heel rubbed. She steeled herself for a walk of shame through the town, resolving to ignore any pointing, staring or name-calling.

But there was none. People were going about their business: some in work clothes, walking purposefully, some ambling with travel mugs. No one took any notice of her, except for a woman who waved and said hello. Jade said hello too, though she had no idea who she was.

The woman grinned. 'It's Betsy, from the bakery,' she said. 'No one recognises me without the apron.'

'Sorry,' said Jade, 'I was miles away.'

She went straight upstairs to the flat, fetched her dressing gown and headed for the shower. The water began to heat up immediately. It had been much better behaved since Jade had taken to keeping a screwdriver on the shelf by the sink.

Once she was scrubbed clean and dressed in a more suitable outfit – a dark-blue top with ruffles at the wrists, a maroon skirt with silver stars and little mirrors on, stripy tights and her Doc Martens – Jade felt much better.

She went downstairs and looked at the shop. It was neat and tidy, as she had straightened up after closing the previous day. Before the trouble had started. *I'll be sad to leave*, she thought.

*Maybe Fi's right and you won't have to.*

*We'll see.* Jade sighed, eyed the *Closed* sign, and left.

She strode down the high street towards Fi's boat, thinking. *Is it the same box as the one Freddy was carrying? Or is it from the same place? Does it even matter?* She was so absorbed that she only saw the person approaching her when he waved and said 'Ms Fitch!'

She jumped, and recognised Inspector Falconer.

'Oh. Hello.' She took a step back.

'I thought you were going to walk straight through me,' said the inspector. 'I was coming to say sorry about last night. At the golf club. I – well, I got a bit carried away.' He was in the navy suit today.

'Mmm,' said Jade. 'I suppose at least you didn't slap handcuffs on me in front of everyone.'

'I really am sorry,' said the inspector. 'This is one of the most frustrating cases I've worked on. Every lead comes to a dead end. That's probably why I got so annoyed with you and your accomplice. I mean friend. But that's no excuse.'

Jade studied him. He did actually look sorry, although it didn't suit him. 'OK,' she said. 'Anyway, did you get my m—'

'Now I've seen you, I'll drop in to the local paper and make sure they understand that any gossip arising from last night is not to be reported.' The inspector mused for a moment, then his brows knitted. 'I'm sorry, what were you saying?'

'Did you get my message about the box?'

'Box? No. What box?'

'Right, come with me. We're going to the boat.'

'Ms Booker's boat?'

'That's the one,' said Jade. She started walking and he fell in step beside her. It was nice to walk alongside someone who didn't either march or meander.

'May I ask you a question?' said the inspector. He

wore a puzzled expression.

'Depends what it is,' said Jade.

'Why are you more dressed up now than you were last night?'

'Reasons,' said Jade, and turned smartly down the cobbled street.

\*\*\*

'So you're sure that this box either bears a close resemblance to the box Freddy was carrying, or it is the actual box,' said Inspector Falconer, eyeing the box with deep suspicion.

'Yes,' said Jade.

He turned to Fi. 'And you're reasonably certain it was this box that the book was in.'

'Yes,' said Fi. 'I'll check with Geraldine, but on my own account, I'm sure.'

'Right,' said the inspector. 'Does this boat have internet access?'

Fi gave him a pained glance. 'Of course it does.'

'Next question. Do you have a computer or a laptop I can borrow? If we can work out where the box came from…'

Fi got up and retrieved her tablet. 'I don't know if you'll be able to access any police databases,' she said.

The inspector raised an eyebrow. 'I was planning to Google it. Ms Fitch, can you describe the stickers you saw on the box?'

Jade closed her eyes and visualised Freddy strolling towards her. Her nose wrinkled and she straightened her face hastily. *Focus on the box...* 'There were lots of small stickers,' she said, 'in primary colours. Red, yellow, blue. Square with rounded corners, like mobile-phone icons. And they had simple black line drawings on. The yellow ones were vases, the blue ones were cups and the red ones had a sort of fountain. That stuck out. Why wouldn't the blue sticker be the fountain?'

'Good question,' said the inspector. 'Probably branding. Where's Google on this thing?'

Fi took it from him and opened the browser. She made to give it back, but the inspector waved a hand. 'You're probably a better typist than I am. Try "red fountain blue cup antique".'

Fi pursed her lips and typed, then hit return. 'We have results.' She scrolled down the list while the others peered at the screen.

'Go up,' said Jade. 'To the images. Look.' She pointed at a logo: a red, a yellow, and a blue square with the images she had described. Underneath were the words *AVOCADO: colourful antiques and collectibles.*

'That's it,' said Fi, and beamed at her.

'But what does it mean?' said the inspector. 'This makes it likely that the box came from Mr Stott's shop, but are there any other businesses in Hazeby or nearby who would also order from this supplier? Or the box might have been left in the back alley for recycling, and someone took it.'

Jade sighed. 'OK, it's not proof, but it's something.'

'Oh, it's definitely something,' said Inspector Falconer. 'Now, who has handled this box since it came into your possession, Ms Booker?'

'Well, I have,' said Fi, 'and Geraldine, obviously.'

'I made it into a box again after it had been flattened,' said Jade. 'But I bet whoever left it wore gloves, just like they did when—'

'When what?' The inspector's eyes narrowed. That suited him much better than looking apologetic.

'I meant just like you would if you were up to no good,' said Jade. 'Will you dust it for fingerprints?'

'Yes,' said the inspector, wearily. 'I don't suppose you have a bag?'

Fi fetched a large paper carrier. 'At this rate I'll have to start charging you for these,' she said. 'Should I put gloves on?'

'Not unless you want to,' said the inspector. 'You've already handled it more than once, and the chance of finding anything on it is slim, but we have to try, and at least discount anyone's that we'd expect to see.' He held the bag open as Fi gently flattened the box and slid it inside. 'Thank you. I'll get this processed and follow up with the company, and you can go back to your businesses. And if you get any brainwaves...' He reached into his breast pocket and handed them each a card. 'This is the number to ring. I don't always answer, but you can leave a message.'

'Don't forget the newspaper office,' said Jade, as he turned to go.

He raised a hand. 'I won't.' He ducked at the entrance and they heard his footsteps on the gangplank, followed by whistling that grew fainter.

'But why would the book have come from Freddy's business?' said Jade. 'The only reason to dump it here would be to plant it on you, and if that was the case, he wouldn't want it back.'

'We won't work it out by sitting here and chewing it over,' said Fi. 'I think much better when I'm busy. Let's get back to work. If we do think of something, we can always get in touch.'

'We can't,' said Jade. 'We don't have each other's numbers.'

'That's easily fixed.' Fi fetched her phone. 'Go on, tell me your number and I'll send you a text.'

Twenty seconds later, Jade's phone pinged. *Hi*, said the message.

*Hi*, she replied.

'There.' Fi slipped her phone in her pocket. 'How ridiculous that we've witnessed a murder and investigated it together, all without knowing each other's phone numbers.'

'Isn't it,' said Jade.

'Right, I'd better get on,' said Fi. 'It's getting close to ten o'clock, and I want to be ready for the river cruiser.'

'Yeah, me too.' Jade stood up and stretched, wishing she didn't have to return to the shop.

'It won't be that bad,' said Fi. 'No one will blame you.'

Jade sighed. 'I'll have to face it some time.' She waved as she left the boat.

Back at the shop, she made a cup of tea and sat at the counter. *I'll open at ten. That's a nice round number. No one's waiting, anyway. I could even leave it till half past.* She thought about putting on one of the CDs she stocked, as she usually did, but couldn't be bothered.

She opened the drawer, pulled out the black notebook with silver stars, and flicked through it. *All the ideas, all the plans I had, all the things I could do...* She found a list of books that customers had asked for. She had drawn three little boxes next to each one. All the left-hand boxes had a tick for *Ordered*, most books had a second box ticked for *Arrived*, and about half had a third tick for *Collected and Paid. Maybe I can return the others.*

Then she heard someone talking in the shop next door. 'Yes, this shop will be available as soon as the current tenant has cleared it out. They have graciously agreed to do that before the end of the notice period. They still have keys, obviously, but they'll hand them in. I believe they've already accepted an offer on their house.'

*Given what I'm paying for this place, you'd think the walls would be thicker,* thought Jade. *Older doesn't mean better built, and money clearly doesn't always buy quality. Look at Freddy's shop.*

'Is the flat upstairs available too?' asked a second person. 'Or is that rented separately?'

'Oh yes, that's available too,' said the first voice. 'The tenant lives elsewhere. I assumed they used it for extra storage, but there is some furniture. A nice double bed, actually.' Jade shuddered.

'Would I be able to see it? I'd be interested in using it for living accommodation.'

'Yes, of course: I have the keys. Would you like to view it now?'

'Please.'

Jade crept upstairs to her flat, holding her breath. *Why have I never heard anything next door before?*

*Because you have music on in the shop. Maybe the flat's got better insulation.*

*I certainly hope so.* Jade put her ear to the wall and listened.

'It's bigger than I thought it would be. Quite light, too.'

'Yes, it's a shame they weren't using it. As far as

anyone knows.' The other person laughed, and the floorboards creaked as they walked about. But Jade had heard enough.

*We thought we were being so careful, Fi and I. We'd meet somewhere nice and private one evening and talk everything over. No wonder Fi got that anonymous note. No wonder they knew what we were doing. They could hear every word we said.*

*It could only be—*

She waited until footsteps descended, then tiptoed downstairs and sat facing the pavement outside Yesteryear Antiquities. A man wearing a leather jacket and jeans emerged, followed by a man in a shiny pale-grey suit. They shook hands, and the letting agent made a *call-me* sign.

*I have to tell Fi.*

Jade waited two more minutes, watching the broomstick creep around the witch clock, then locked up and ran.

# CHAPTER 24

It was hard for Fi to serve customers, waiting for the moment she'd be free to follow up what Jade had discovered. She'd had an idea which might bear fruit, if only she could leave the boat long enough.

When Nerys appeared, her face a little anxious, Fi's heart leapt. But when she checked the clock and saw that it was nowhere near twelve, it sank again. Had Nerys come to say that she'd decided to stop working almost as soon as she'd started?

'Hi,' said Fi, bracing herself for the inevitable. 'You're early.'

'I thought you might be glad of extra help today. Is that right?'

'Did someone say so?'

'Oh, well, I mean… Everyone knows it's hard at the moment, with all the fuss and nosiness, and we do care, and I could do with the cash, but if I've got it wrong…'

'Oh!' Fi breathed a sigh of relief. Stuart must have bumped into Nerys and put it forward as a suggestion. She wasn't going to argue. 'Thanks so much. Is it OK if I go out now? I'll try not to be long. If anyone comes looking for me, you've got my number.'

'Yeah, of course.'

What Fi wanted to do wouldn't take long. As she wheeled her bicycle onto the towpath she thought of texting Jade, but Jade didn't need any distractions from opening the shop and facing her fears.

She cycled through town until she reached the shop Wendy Stott volunteered at. It supported a small local charity, and Fi frequently scouted it for possible stock. Sometimes, if they were there at the same time, Fi would pick Wendy's brains about gardening on the deck of the book barge. There would be nothing more natural than for her to do it today, while repeating her condolences, then mention that she was thinking of including bric-a-brac on the boat and wondered where Freddy had sourced his. *We need proof of a link.*

A small voice whispered, *Text Jade, or you're doing exactly what you had a go at her for last night.* She argued back: *It's not the same.* The small voice continued to mutter as she chained up her bike, and Fi felt uneasy.

In the shop, Wendy was nowhere to be seen. Perhaps she was in the stockroom. Fi went to the counter. 'Is Wendy in today?' she asked the woman behind the till. 'I hoped to distract her a bit by asking about creating a herb garden—'

'Sorry, love,' said the assistant. 'She's given up.'

'Given up what?'

'Working here. I think all the pity over Freddy sticks in her throat. She's moving abroad.'

'When did she decide that?'

'First I heard was when I came in at nine thirty. It'll be worse for her to lose that garden than him, don't you reckon?'

'Mmm.' Fi's sense of unease increased.

'You could go round and see if she'll give you a plant as a souvenir, and do us a favour at the same time.'

'A favour?'

'Wendy left her thermal mug behind. It'll save her coming for it.'

'Oh, right. Yes, of course.'

Fi left, put the things in her panniers and unlocked the bike. *OK, OK,* she told the small voice, then texted Jade.

*Going to Wendy's house for plants. If she has a box to put them in, or I can find out about F's suppliers, we might be on to something. Back by 11 but if not, come and get me. Still can't remember house number but our mutual friend should know.*

It was a short cycle to Wendy's home and when

222

she arrived, Fi realised why she couldn't remember the number. There was simply a name on the gate: *Stott Acres*, as if it was a good deal grander than a house identical to five others in the road, with a third of an acre of garden, if that.

No one was about, and all the other houses were behind high hedges and fences. There was nothing for it.

Fi wheeled her bicycle through the gate and propped it near the arched ironwork gateway which led down the side of the house to the garden. No one was in the two rooms on either side of the front door, so she rang the doorbell and waited.

After what felt like an age, Wendy opened the door a crack and peered round. 'Fi! How nice to see you. Aren't you working?' Her friendly words and anxious expression didn't quite match.

'Morning off,' said Fi. 'I heard you're planning to go abroad and thought I'd pop round.'

'Don't you just love town gossip.'

Fi gave a rueful smile. 'I wouldn't want you to go without saying goodbye. I went to the charity shop and they said—'

'I hope you won't offer your condolences again.' Wendy clenched her jaw. 'I'm sick of everyone's pity.'

'I can offer you this,' said Fi, handing over the thermal mug, 'and if you're up to it, pick your brains about—'

'About what?' Wendy's voice was sharp.

'About plants in pots. Herbs. Perennial flowering, um…'

Wendy's pale face cleared. 'I'd offered to help with your deck garden. I'd forgotten. I'll make us coffee and we can chat in the drawing room – that's what Freddy used to call it. I call it the back sitting room.'

'Lovely. Thanks.'

Fi followed Wendy into a room full of dark oak furniture, old oil paintings and a sea of fiddly ornaments, and sat on a moss-green velour sofa.

'The kettle's just boiled,' said Wendy. 'Is instant all right? Milk? Sugar?'

'Instant's fine. Milk please, no sugar.'

Fi watched Wendy leave then looked through the large French windows. The sun shone on the pretty garden with its floral borders, blossoming shrubs and a path winding round a little brick shed that Wendy had turned into a feature. Lovely as it was, it couldn't compensate for the heavy atmosphere in the house. She picked up her phone to text Jade and gazed around her. On the mantlepiece, sympathy cards had been jammed haphazardly between mismatched china, forcing a photograph to tip forward. Fi went to set it upright. It was the Stotts' wedding photograph from what looked like forty years earlier. The glass had smashed, scratching Freddy's face. Something told Fi to leave it face down and scurry back to the sofa. Coming here had been a very bad idea.

'Here you are,' said Wendy, putting the mugs on the coffee table. 'Once you've drunk that, I'll take you through to the other sitting room – Freddy called it the library – and you can choose some books for your shop. I shan't be taking all of them. Then I'll get my sketch pad and we'll discuss gardening ideas.'

'Thank you.'

'The coffee won't be too hot, I made it nice and milky.'

Fi contemplated the mug. The drink was dark and murky, as if Wendy had put in at least three teaspoons of coffee. 'I burnt my tongue earlier, so it's a bit sensitive,' she lied, wishing she could text someone surreptitiously. 'I'll let it cool. I, er… You'll miss your garden.'

Wendy got up and half-pulled the curtains. 'I'm not sure I can bear it.' There was a tremor in her voice. 'After the children grew up and emigrated, I put my heart and soul into it. They hardly ever visit. They both said they'd return for the funeral, but what about now? What about me? The plants are a better family. But I can make another garden somewhere else, can't I?' Her voice was wistful, then she fixed Fi with a stare. 'I'm sure your coffee is cool enough. Do drink up.'

Fi racked her brain for a reason to get outside, then as far away as possible. 'I, er… I like what you've done with the shed. Could I—'

'Every old garden has a shed. What does it have to do with you? Oh, I remember: I did start a plan for your deck. Drink up and we'll—'

The doorbell rang and someone hammered on the front door. Wendy fell silent, her fists clenched. She didn't move.

'Shall *I* go?' suggested Fi.

'Don't be ridiculous.' Wendy marched from the room, pulling the door closed.

The bell sounded again, followed by more hammering. Fi got to her feet and opened the inner door but Wendy was there, holding a large knife. 'Sit down,' she muttered. She jabbed the knife at Fi's throat, grabbed her arm and pushed her into the nearest chair. 'Sit and be quiet until they go away.'

'Wh—' The blade of the knife touched Fi's skin. She wanted to scream, but she didn't dare move the muscles in her throat.

'Do you think I don't know that you and your friend have been snooping?' Wendy whispered. 'I suspected you'd come looking for me today. I saw Nerys at the minimart and hinted that I'd heard you were struggling. I knew she'd go along to help, from nosiness if nothing else, and then you wouldn't be able to resist snooping some more and I could deal with you. If Nerys remembers it was me who suggested it, I'll say your friend told me you needed help.'

The hammering stopped. The blade quivered against Fi's throat but it wasn't pressing so hard and Wendy was watching the door, clearly listening. If Fi leaned backwards, perhaps she could twist, perhaps she could grab Wendy's wrist...

There was an almighty smash. Despite the blade at her throat, Fi turned instinctively to the French windows and so did Wendy. The curtains were moving...

With a tiny gasp, Wendy dropped the knife and reached for Fi's coffee.

'Oh no you don't,' said Fi, knocking it out of her hand. Coffee spilled across the table and Inspector Falconer stormed through the French windows. Then she heard the crunch of wood as the front door gave way. A constable dashed into the room, followed by Jade.

Wendy's eyes darted from person to person, then she dropped onto the sofa and put her head in her hands.

'He said he'd applied for a divorce,' she said, in a low, cold voice. 'He said that because I've never earned a salary and put money into the household, I had no right to anything. Not even a penny in maintenance. He said I'd have to move out and leave my garden to be ruined by that – that woman – and he didn't care what happened to me. I'm sixty-four. I didn't know what to do. And the children don't care, either. All my life he's picked at my intelligence and my looks and my figure and my cooking and the children learned to copy him. I-I just wanted to stay in my house with my garden.' She heaved a sob.

'Wendy Stott,' said the inspector, very gently, 'you do not have to say anything. But it may harm your defence if you do not mention when questioned something which you later rely on in court. Anything you do say may be given in evidence. I am arresting you for the murder of your husband, Freddy Stott, and for the assault on Fi Booker. Is there anything you want to say before we take you into custody? Anything we ought to know about that coffee, or anything else in this house?'

Wendy's shoulders drooped. For a moment, Fi thought she would refuse to speak, but then she said in that low, monotone voice, 'I don't care any more. I thought if he was gone it would be over, but he's...' She waved her hand at the furnishings. 'He's *everywhere*. He's still bullying me, even after he's dead.'

Against her better judgement, Fi sat beside her. 'What happened next, Wendy?'

Wendy took a breath. 'I found an antique curiosity under the brick floor of the old shed a few months ago. A tin of rat poison – Victorian, perhaps. Freddy would just have laughed if I'd shown him, so I put it

228

back, meaning to find out how to dispose of it. I completely forgot about it until he told me I'd have to leave.'

'And then?' said the inspector.

'It was the last straw. No one would suspect mousy old uneducated me could do anything with chemicals. Roger Reilly could, Frank Menzies could, snooty old Darcy could. You'd think it was one of them, wouldn't you? But none of them would ever be convicted. Not in the end. You'd decide Fi had been accidentally landed with a book poisoned a hundred years ago and Freddy was the unlucky one who bought it. In the end, you'd just put it down to bad luck.'

'Analysis showed those pages were recently poisoned,' said Inspector Falconer.

'Oh,' said Wendy.

'Where did you get it?'

'It was my grandfather's. He used to do magic tricks from it for me. It was *his* grandfather's, I imagine. My children were never interested, so I kept it with my other childhood things, to remind me of happier times. Freddy mentioned it once or twice, but if I'd given it to him, he'd have sold it in his wretched shop. I told him I'd given it to a cousin years ago and it had been lost in a house move. It hurt to damage the book with poison, but then I remembered my grandfather couldn't bear bullies, so it was a way of making sure he protected me one last time.'

Wendy paused and looked into the middle distance, as if remembering the moment when she made the decision to poison the book. To poison her husband. A journey of no return. 'I dropped the books at the barge one night, then told Freddy that I'd seen a copy of *More Magic* there. I mentioned that I'd heard it had a very interesting chapter on a spell for virility in the middle. He never listened to me properly, so if he lived, he'd never remember that it was I who'd told him. And that was where it went a bit wrong. Because *I* told him, he wasn't really listening. I'd thought he'd go that day to get it. I had to check it was on display, then remind him. The quicker he got it, the less risk that anyone else would be in danger.'

'Except Ms Booker or her assistant.'

'Oh, but the *outside* was safe,' insisted Wendy. 'And I knew Fi and Geraldine would treat it carefully. Freddy was meant to buy it and be so impatient that he'd lick his fingers in that disgusting way he had and flick through the pages to *that* chapter so that he could keep up with that – that *woman*. He might sit on a bench to read it. That would be the end of him, before he'd even got back to his shop, and no one would ever have linked it to me.'

Wendy stopped talking and focused on the room. She looked at Fi's neck and gasped. Fi put up her hand and felt a tiny trickle of blood. She swallowed.

'Found this, guv,' said a constable, entering the

room with an evidence bag. Inside was what appeared to be an old metal box with a picture of a mouse on it. No, not a mouse. A rat. Through the plastic Fi saw the box's stained cream label, with words in red, *RAT REVENGE: STRYCHNINE – POISON*, and a red skull and crossbones.

Fi stared at it, then at the constable pouring coffee from her mug into an evidence container. She was aware of Inspector Falconer watching, his face grim, and Jade's hand on her arm. The room started to swim and the edges of her vision went totally black.

The last thing she heard before she passed out was Wendy's plaintive voice. 'If only you two hadn't interfered…'

# CHAPTER 25

'So you can't tell us what happened at the Stotts' house?' asked the customer, with a disappointed face.

'I'm afraid not,' said Jade. 'It might pervert the course of justice.'

'That's so unfair,' murmured one of the young women who had asked Jade about under-the-counter merchandise. Jade couldn't remember whether she had been the one on the left or the right. In any case, she seemed perfectly happy leafing through a copy of *Twilight: Midnight Sun*.

'It would be unfair of me to spill the beans when the police worked so hard to resolve the case,' said Jade.

'Come off it,' said the former assistant from Freddy's shop. 'We all read the local paper. We all know that you and Fi from the book boat were involved.'

'In that case, you don't need me to fill in the details, do you?' Jade grinned at their stricken faces. 'If you're buying, you'd better come up now. I'm closing for lunch in five minutes.'

'About that,' said Freddy's ex-assistant, sidling up to the till. 'Are you looking for an assistant? I've got experience.'

*In talking on the phone and filing your nails*, thought Jade, but smiled at her anyway. *As if I can afford an assistant.* 'We'll see,' she said. 'What was Freddy paying you, if you don't mind me asking?'

'Minimum wage,' said the girl. 'And I'm nineteen, so that's £6.83 an hour.'

'I appreciate your honesty,' said Jade. Cogs turned in her brain. *I could get her to cover lunchtimes, or I could take an afternoon off once a week. Maybe even two.* The thought astonished her. She had never, except when she was unemployed, had a free afternoon in the week to call her own. 'Can I take your name and number and I'll have a think.' She opened her notebook to a fresh page.

The girl scrawled her name and number and Jade peered at it. 'What does that say?'

'Netta,' she mumbled.

'That's unusual.'

'Mmm,' said Netta, in a way that suggested she didn't want to talk about it. Someone coughed behind her and she glared at them, then shuffled out of the way.

Jade dealt with the purchasers, then shooed everyone from the shop. As they left, the *Twilight* woman whispered to Netta, 'I heard she used her powers.' They saw her looking and scurried off. Laughing, Jade turned the sign to *Closed* and under it stuck a note that said: *Out to lunch. Back at 2.*

She strolled along, enjoying the sunshine on her face and the slight breeze. Several people said hello to her, most of whom she didn't know. *What it is to be a minor celebrity.*

The local rag had made her and Fi front-page news. *LOCAL TRADERS FIGHT CRIME*, the headline shouted, with a photo of Jade and Fi flanking Inspector Falconer – Inspector Marcus Falconer, as it turned out – and smiling. The article itself had been circumspect, limiting itself to the facts of Freddy Stott's murder, until it made reference to *the thrilling arrest of a suspect in broad daylight, made with the assistance of the plucky pair.* The article had also, very considerately, mentioned both Fi's and Jade's businesses by name and said where they could be found. An interview on the Hazeby FM breakfast show had followed, during which Jade had happened to mention that her shop sold good-luck charms and protective spells. She had had to buy extra stock as a result.

*Maybe I could get an assistant*, she thought, as she

entered the cobbled street. She saw two people leave the boat, talking and carrying a large paper bag each. *Fi is doing well, too.*

She entered the barge, where Fi's new helper, Nerys, was writing in a notebook. 'Hello there,' said Jade.

'Just a minute,' said Nerys. 'Let me finish this first.' She carried on writing, then put her pen down. 'Sorry. If I don't write what's been sold, I completely forget. I don't know whether I'm coming or going.'

'I'm sure it'll be fine,' said Jade.

'Maybe,' said Nerys. 'I swear my brain isn't the same since having kids. In one ear and out the other. You haven't got anything in your shop that would improve my memory, have you?'

Jade smiled. 'I doubt it. Is Fi about?'

As she spoke, the door to Fi's quarters swung open and Fi came in, wearing a floral shift dress and sandals.

'I hope you haven't dressed up for me,' said Jade. 'We're only going to the pub.'

Fi shrugged. 'It's still a lunch date.' She turned to Nerys. 'We'll be at the Duck and Druid. You can always ring me if you need to ask me anything. You've got my number, haven't you?'

Nerys picked up the pen. 'Can I take Jade's, too? Better safe than sorry.'

\*\*\*

'This is nice,' said Fi, gazing around her as they headed up to the high street. 'Lunch away from the boat with an actual person, sitting down.'

'I know,' said Jade. 'How's Nerys working out for you? And what happened to the other assistant, the one who was away? Geraldine, was it?'

Fi made a face. 'She came back from her retreat and the minute she stepped into the boat, told me it was ruining her energy and giving her bad vibes.'

'Bad vibes, eh? So has she left?'

'She's thinking it over,' said Fi. 'I'm surprised she hasn't visited your shop for incense and salt, or whatever you use to cleanse vibes.'

'Don't ask me,' said Jade. 'Give me her description and I'll look out for her. See if I can persuade her that it's all in her mind.'

Fi wrinkled her nose and flapped a dismissive hand. 'Nerys will be fine with a bit more practice.'

Jade glanced at her. 'Aren't you laid-back?'

Fi considered this. 'Maybe I am,' she said. 'After what we've been through lately, a stroppy assistant is nothing to get wound up about, is it?'

'I'll drink to that,' said Jade. 'And here we are.'

They entered the pub and walked up to the bar. Jade sensed people looking at her, but in a good way. 'I've booked a table for two,' Fi told the barman.

'Excellent,' he said, beaming at them. 'If you'd like to come this way.' He took them to a window table, waited for them to sit, and handed them each a menu. 'I'll be back in a few minutes to take your drinks orders.'

'The VIP treatment,' said Jade, once he had left. 'I could get used to this. Maybe we should solve crimes more often.'

'No thanks,' said Fi, grimacing. 'Once is more than enough. Poor Wendy. When you think of what Freddy did to her…'

'True,' said Jade, 'but she led us a merry dance. Not to mention throwing suspicion on anyone who'd ever worked with chemicals and had dealings with Freddy.'

Fi laughed. 'It's been quite an introduction to the town for you.' She leaned forward. 'Will you stay?'

Jade put down her menu. 'Well, now that Inspector Falconer has stopped regarding me as public enemy number one…'

'Don't be silly. He was just doing his job.'

'Mmm.' Jade had a sudden vision of the inspector in his tuxedo advancing towards her in the golf-club foyer, stern as could be. If she hadn't been worried sick, it would have been rather thrilling. 'Yes, I expect I'll stay,' she said, picking up her menu again. 'Apart from anything else, the shop's on a six-month lease.'

Fi laughed. 'And you're raking it in.'

Jade grinned. 'You're not doing so badly yourself, young lady.'

A floorboard nearby creaked and the barman approached, holding two champagne flutes. 'A complimentary glass of prosecco as a small token of our appreciation, ladies. It's nice to have the town back to normal.'

'Gosh,' said Fi. 'Thank you.'

'Indeed,' said Jade, feeling her cheeks glow.

'Are you ready to order yet?' he asked.

'If you could give us a couple of minutes,' said Fi.

'Of course.' He retreated.

'I could definitely get used to this,' said Jade. She picked up a glass. 'What shall we drink to? Absent friends?'

Fi screwed her face up. 'That reminds me of Freddy. Business success?'

Jade shook her head. 'Too dull. How about new beginnings?'

'That'll do.' Fi raised her glass. 'To new beginnings!'

They clinked glasses and Jade mused, as she sipped her prosecco, that perhaps this time she had landed on her feet.

# WHAT TO READ NEXT

If you've enjoyed reading Fi and Jade's first investigation together, watch out for the next book in the series: *Death on Opening Night.*

When sixties movie star Tallulah Levantine moves to Hazeby-on-Wyvern to star in a production of *Macbeth*, she becomes the target of deadly threats. Rehearsals are plagued with accidents and a body is found in her dressing room.

With the help of her friend Fi, Jade Fitch sets out to discover the murderer lurking in the wings before it's too late.

Check out *Death on Opening Night* at https://mybook.to/OpeningNight.

If you've enjoyed reading a co-written book, Caster and Fleet Mysteries is a six-book series we wrote together, set in 1890s London. Meet Katherine and

Connie, two young women who become friends in the course of solving a mystery together. Their unlikely partnership takes them to the music hall, masked balls, and beyond. Expect humour, a touch of romance, and above all, shenanigans!

The first book in the series is *The Case of the Black Tulips,* and you can read all about it here: http://mybook.to/Tulips.

If you love modern cozy mysteries set in rural England, Pippa Parker Mysteries is another six-book series set in and around the village of Much Gadding.

In the first book, *Murder at the Playgroup*, Pippa is a reluctant newcomer to the village. When she meets the locals, she's absolutely sure. There's just one problem; she's eight months pregnant.

The village is turned upside down when a pillar of the community is found dead at Gadding Goslings playgroup. No one could have murdered her except the people who were there. Everyone's a suspect, including Pippa...

With a baby due any minute, and hampered by her toddler son, can Pippa unmask the murderer?

Find *Murder at the Playgroup* here: http://mybook.to/playgroup.

Finally, if you love books and magic, welcome to the Magical Bookshop! This six-book series combines mystery, magic, cats and of course books, and is set in modern London.

When Jemma James takes a job at Burns Books, the second-worst secondhand bookshop in London, she finds her ambition to turn it around thwarted at every step. Raphael, the owner, is more interested in his newspaper than sales. Folio the bookshop cat has it in for Jemma, and the shop itself appears to have a mind of its own. Or is it more than that?

The first in the series, *Every Trick in the Book*, is here: http://mybook.to/bookshop1

# ACKNOWLEDGEMENTS

As ever, our first thanks go to our wonderful beta readers – Carol Bissett, Ruth Cunliffe, Christine Downes, Stephen Lenhardt, Carmen Radtke and Julia Smith – and to our keen-eyed and knowledgeable proofreader, John Croall. Thank you so much for your feedback, corrections and suggestions! Any errors that remain are our responsibility.

Having enjoyed writing the Caster & Fleet Victorian mystery series together, we'd said for a while that we would be up for collaborating again one day, when the time was right. We discussed it again in summer 2022, when we met up in London. As it happened, we were staying on a barge moored near Canary Wharf... So we need to say a huge thank you to our host Inigo for inadvertently giving us ideas! Fi's boat *Coralie* isn't exactly the same as Inigo's, though – his was, thankfully, murder-free!

Another inspiration for *Coralie* is the wonderful Word on the Water book boat in London. Check it out here: https://wordonthewater.co.uk.

And finally, many thanks to you, the reader. We hope you've enjoyed this first book in the Booker & Fitch mystery series, and if you have, please consider leaving a short review or a rating on Amazon and/or Goodreads. Reviews and ratings are immensely important to authors, as they help books to find new readers.

# COVER CREDITS

Image: Depositphotos.

**Cover fonts:**

Fairing by Design and Co.

Dancing Script OT by Impallari Type: https://www.fontsquirrel.com/fonts/dancing-script-ot. License: SIL Open Font License v1.10: http://scripts.sil.org/OFL.

# ABOUT LIZ HEDGECOCK

Liz Hedgecock grew up in London, England, did an English degree, and then took forever to start writing. After several years working in the National Health Service, some short stories crept into the world. A few even won prizes. Then the stories started to grow longer...

Now Liz travels between the nineteenth and twenty-first centuries, murdering people. To be fair, she does usually clean up after herself.

Liz's reimaginings of Sherlock Holmes, her Pippa Parker cozy mystery series, the Caster & Fleet Victorian mystery series (with Paula Harmon), the Magical Bookshop series, and the Maisie Frobisher Mysteries are available in ebook and paperback.

Liz lives in Cheshire with her husband and two sons, and when she's not writing or child-wrangling you can usually find her reading, messing about on

Twitter, or cooing over stuff in museums and art galleries. That's her story, anyway, and she's sticking to it.

Website/blog: http://lizhedgecock.wordpress.com
Facebook: http://www.facebook.com/
lizhedgecockwrites
Twitter: http://twitter.com/lizhedgecock
Goodreads: https://www.goodreads.com/lizhedgecock

# ABOUT PAULA HARMON

Paula Harmon is a civil servant, living in Dorset, married with two adult children. Paula has several writing projects underway and wonders where the housework fairies are, because the house is a mess and she can't think why.

For book news, offers and even the occasional recipe, please sign up to my newsletter via my website.

https://paulaharmon.com
viewauthor.at/PHAuthorpage
https://www.facebook.com/pg/paulaharmonwrites
https://www.goodreads.com/paula_harmon
https://twitter.com/Paula_S_Harmon

# BOOKS BY LIZ HEDGECOCK

To check out any of my books, please visit my Amazon author page at http://author.to/LizH. If you follow me there, you'll be notified whenever I release a new book.

### The Magical Bookshop (6 novels)
An eccentric owner, a hostile cat, and a bookshop with a mind of its own. Can Jemma turn around the second-worst secondhand bookshop in London? And can she learn its secrets?

### Pippa Parker Mysteries (6 novels)
Meet Pippa Parker: mum, amateur sleuth, and resident of a quaint English village called Much Gadding. And then the murders began…

### Caster & Fleet Mysteries (6 novels, with Paula Harmon)
There's a new detective duo in Victorian London . . . and they're women! Meet Katherine and Connie, two young women who become partners in crime. Solving it, that is!

**Mrs Hudson & Sherlock Holmes** (3 novels)
Mrs Hudson is Sherlock Holmes's elderly landlady. Or is she? Find out her real story here.

**Maisie Frobisher Mysteries** (4 novels)
When Maisie Frobisher, a bored young Victorian socialite, goes travelling in search of adventure, she finds more than she could ever have dreamt of. Mystery, intrigue and a touch of romance.

**Sherlock & Jack** (3 novellas)
Jack has been ducking and diving all her life. But when she meets the great detective Sherlock Holmes they form an unlikely partnership. And Jack discovers that she is more important than she ever realised…

**Halloween Sherlock** (3 novelettes)
Short dark tales of Sherlock Holmes and Dr Watson, perfect for a grim winter's night.

### For children
*A Christmas Carrot* (with Zoe Harmon)
*Perkins the Halloween Cat* (with Lucy Shaw)
*Rich Girl, Poor Girl* (for 9-12 year olds)

# BOOKS BY PAULA HARMON

THE MURDER BRITANNICA SERIES
Murder Mysteries set in 2nd Century Britain
mybook.to/MurderBritanniaSeries

THE MARGARET DEMERAY SERIES
Historical Mysteries set in the lead-up to World War 1
mybook.to/MargaretDemeraySeries

OTHER BOOKS BY PAULA HARMON
https://paulaharmon.com/books-by-paula-harmon/

SHORT STORIES BY PAULA HARMON & VAL
PORTELLI
viewbook.at/PHWeirdandpeculiartales

AUDIOBOOKS BY PAULA HARMON
https://paulaharmon.com/audiobooks/

WHITE
RHINO
BOOKS

Printed in Great Britain
by Amazon

21347148R00150